Until We Say Love

SHORT STORIES ON FLEETING MOMENTS AND SECOND CHANCES

SHIRLEY SIATON

INKY
SWORD

A Note for the Reader

These love stories are a celebration of hope, the magic of fleeting moments, and the profound comfort of a second chance. Each tale is crafted to lead to a happy or hopeful ending, but as in life, the paths our characters walk are not always easy.

For your care and consideration, I wanted to provide a gentle heads-up on some of the heavier emotional themes you will encounter within these pages.

Please be aware that this collection includes:

- Grief following the death of a loved one from accidents or illness
- Past infidelity and emotional/financial betrayal by a partner
- Major medical procedures (specifically a heart transplant) and survivor's guilt
- Brief mentions of parental abandonment and a chronically ill parent

Thank you for opening your heart to *Until We Say Love*. Please read kindly and look after yourself.

For all those who believe their story isn't over.

For every heart that waits for the spring,
and for the love that proves it's never too late to bloom.

CONTENTS

Until We Say Love

CHAPTER 1

The Morning Commute

THE BUS ALWAYS SMELLS FAINTLY OF COFFEE AND rain.

Even when it hasn't rained. Even when I have already finished the coffee in my trusty steel flask.

And I don't know his name.

Not for months.

But I know his routine as well as my own.

He boards at the second stop after mine. He takes the same seat, third row from the back, by the window. He always rests his bag between his feet.

I've grown familiar with the way he tilts his head slightly when reading something on his phone. His eyes have a faint golden-brown glow whenever they catch the morning sun.

His hair is longish and impossibly thick. He has a habit of running a hand through it whenever the traffic barely budges in the bus lane.

And he smiles at me whenever he catches me staring.

Like an idiot, I always smile back. Depending on my day, I sometimes throw in a nod.

That's all we ever do.

The world outside is usually a blur of billboards, puddles, and students dragging heavy backpacks, but inside, time feels different whenever he's there.

My time on the bus somehow feels measured, contained in our own little world. As if we're all part of the same little ritual before the city swallows us whole.

Every morning we exist together like this. Parallel, smiling, but never touching.

It happens on a Tuesday.

The bus is unusually crowded. People stand shoulder to shoulder, muttering apologies, holding onto metal poles as the driver lurches us forward.

When I step in, my usual seat is gone. So is the backup seat, and the backup to the backup. The only spot left is next to him.

I hesitate, heart racing like I've been caught doing something illegal. But the driver honks, the aisle clogs, and my choices vanish. I slide into the seat, trying not to breathe too loudly.

He glances up from his phone, surprise flickering in his eyes.

But then he smiles. Not the polite kind, but the kind that belongs only to me.

"Hi," he says. His voice is lower than I expected. It's calm, almost soothing.

"Hi," I echo, clutching my oversized tote to my chest like a shield.

"It's gonna be a long ride today," he says, nodding toward the packed aisle.

"Yeah," I say. "Guess we'll have to survive it together."

His laugh is small but genuine. "Guess so."

It isn't much. Just a few syllables each, but it's enough to make the ride feel different. Enough to make me wish the traffic was worse.

❧

After that morning, something changes.

We don't talk every day, not at first. But some mornings, when the bus feels less like a coffin and more like a coffee shop, we speak.

He tells me his name is Santi. He works at an architecture firm half a block away from his stop. He spends his days trapped in meetings and his nights sketching on napkins or receipt paper because "ideas never show up on schedule."

I tell him I'm Gina. I work at a publishing house, mostly behind the scenes, making sure commas behave and deadlines don't explode. I share a love-hate relationship with my red pen, but it's the very thing that has gotten me places.

We swap mundane fragments of our lives.

"My landlady feeds all the strays in our street," I tell him.

"Cats?" he asks.

"Dogs. Six of them. They bark like a choir every morning."

He grins. "Better than an alarm clock."

"Why architecture?" I ask one morning.

"Because buildings don't move," he says. Then, in a softer voice, he adds, "Unlike people."

He asks about the books I carry sometimes. I ask about the playlist that leaks faintly from his headphones when he forgets to lower the volume.

Our conversations are stitched together from the small, the ordinary, the kind of details you don't tell strangers.

Because we're not strangers anymore.

Then, one Monday, he doesn't get on.

Tuesday, the seat is empty again.

Wednesday, still no Santi.

I tell myself it's silly to notice. People change routines. People oversleep. People have real lives outside my narrow hour of the morning.

But his absence feels…wrong. My stop feels heavier. The ride feels endless.

By Thursday, I stop looking at the window. I keep a book open but never read a line. I bite my lip until it hurts.

On Friday, I step onto the bus, preparing myself for another empty space.

And then he's there.

Third row from the back, hair messier than usual, tie knotted badly, eyes shadowed. Relief floods me so strongly I almost laugh out loud.

I sit beside him before I can stop myself.

"You disappeared," I say, a little too quickly and accusingly.

He looks guilty. "Work trip. Last minute. I should have said something."

"You don't owe me that," I say quickly, but I know my voice betrays me.

He studies me for a second.

After a while, he says softly, "You noticed."

"Of course I noticed," I admit, heat rushing to my cheeks. "You're…" I falter as my brain searches frantically for an explanation. "You're part of my mornings."

He smiles. "You're part of mine, too, Gina."

And that's the first time I realize I've been holding my breath all week.

The next Friday, the sky falls apart.

Rain pours so heavily it feels like the bus is sailing instead of driving. Everyone boards drenched, umbrellas dripping, shoes squeaking.

At his stop, Santi slides in beside me, shirt damp at the shoulders. A drop of rain clings stubbornly to his hair.

Without thinking, I reach into my tote and pull out a tissue. "Here."

He takes it, brushing the water away. "Thanks."

"You're dripping on my sleeve," I say lightly.

"You're complaining," he says right back, "but you haven't moved away."

"Maybe I don't mind."

Despite the weather, he gives me a broad, sunny grin.

The bus rattles over a puddle, throwing us against each other for a moment, shoulder to shoulder, knee to knee. My pulse forgets how to count.

The storm roars outside, but inside, it's strangely quiet.

"I'd miss you," I say suddenly, my throat almost catching at the suddenness of the admission.

He turns to look at me closely. "What?"

"If you weren't here," I murmur, a blush rising from my collar. "If you stopped taking this bus. I'd miss you."

There's a long pause. His eyes light up, then shimmer.

I don't know what he's thinking. All I know is that he doesn't stop staring at me.

"I'd miss you, too," he says softly. "I'd really miss you."

The windows blur. The bus keeps moving.

But I feel something change.

Something seems to snap into place, unable to let go.

Weeks later, he finally says it, one drizzling morning.

As the bus nears my stop, he fidgets too noticeably, then finally says, "Dinner?"

His voice is steady, but his eyes aren't. They flick from my face to a spot above my shoulder.

"Dinner?" I echo.

"Off the bus," he clarifies, smiling nervously. "Some place real. I think we're overdue."

My heart kicks against my ribs.

"Yes," I say. "Definitely."

The bus rattles to a halt at my stop.

Passengers push into the aisle, umbrellas colliding, voices spilling out into the drizzle.

Santi steps down first, then turns back with his hand held out, waiting for me. When I take it and join him on the slick pavement, he leans closer. The rain threads between us, soft and silver.

For a moment, the whole gray, wet city feels hushed.

And then he kisses me.

It tastes like rain and coffee. It carries the weight and memory of every morning that brought us to this moment.

When he pulls back, he reaches for my cheek, brushing a damp, errant strand of my hair away.

"I'm glad you sat beside me that day," he says quietly.

"So am I," I answer.

Behind us, the bus pulls away, obedient to its route. But

we walk in the other direction, away from the stop, toward something that feels a lot like home.

Months from now, maybe years, I'll still think of the first morning we spoke.

Of umbrellas dripping ghosts and memories onto the floor. Of tissues brushing away the rain.

Of glances and smiles louder than the traffic.

The bus still smells like coffee and rain.

But now, it smells like a story.

A story from something as everyday as the routine of two people making their way through a rain-drenched city.

A story of love that began with a morning commute.

CHAPTER 2

The Light in the Window

I DON'T KNOW WHO HE IS.

I don't even know what he does for a living.

Not for the first three months, anyway.

But I know that he makes coffee at exactly 6:04 every morning. I know that he reads by the window with his feet curled under him like a cat. I know that he waters his plants every three days, even if it rains. I know that he leaves his window open during thunderstorms, but unrolls a makeshift tarp to keep the wind and water out.

And I know that his lamp glows until almost midnight, flicking off a few seconds before mine.

I don't mean to watch. Not at first. I only notice because his apartment is across from mine—diagonal, close enough to see into when the curtains are open, far enough that the details blur.

He's quiet, almost gentle, by nature. He doesn't play loud music or have people over. He moves like he doesn't want to bother the floor.

In a city that's crowded, loud, and constantly moving, his quiet is magnetic.

I call him Window Boy in my head.

Window Boy with his thick black hair almost always tousled, with his slightly lopsided silver-rimmed glasses.

I know how he looks the same way I know my favorite digital print.

The first time we acknowledge each other, it's barely more than a glance. Or maybe a blink exchange.

I'm standing by my kitchen counter with a bowl of noodles. It's almost midnight. I look up, and he's at his window, watching the rain.

He sees me.

I see him.

We freeze at the same time.

A heartbeat of stillness.

Then, shyly, he lifts his hand. He gives me a small, tentative wave.

I wave back.

He smiles. Just a little.

Just enough.

That night, I sleep better than I have in weeks.

We fall into a rhythm.

We wave in the mornings now. I sip my awful green tea, he sips coffee.

Sometimes I hold up a book, and he nods like he approves.

Once, he held up a notebook with a post-it stuck to it that said, *"What are you reading today?"*

I wrote my answer on printer paper and held it up. *"Never Let Me Go, Kazuo Ishiguro."*

He made a little heart with his hands.

I decide he's a little bit of a nerd, just like me.

It was stupid. And sweet.

It made my whole day quieter in the best way.

If this is peace, then I want it.

I learn his habits. He likes chicken-flavored instant noodles with egg. He folds laundry with perfect corners, always starting with the largest pieces. He takes his time drinking his coffee, inhaling and sipping in turn, causing his glasses to fog up.

He learns mine too. He knows when I'm working late. He knows when I'm too tired to cook and eat crackers at the window instead. He knows when I'm sad, even if I'm smiling.

I can tell because he sends a small, thoughtful gesture across the distance. Sometimes it's a thumbs up or a peace sign; other times it's a paper swan or a slightly wilted flower stuck to the glass.

I keep a journal now, a weird little A4 document online that I update every day before bed. The template is a rich pink, bordered with white hearts and fluffy cats.

Day 42: He wore blue again. The good blue. The soft one.

Day 55: We both held up ramen at the same time. It felt like a conversation.

Day 61: He waved goodnight. I waved back late. He waited. He didn't even move from his spot.

I don't write about work. Or my family. Or my loneliness. I only write about him.

One night, the storm hits hard.

The kind that knocks power out in entire blocks with one strong gust.

My apartment goes dark. I scramble for candles. For a moment, the city feels swallowed.

I move to the window out of habit.

His apartment is dark too.

But then, a flashlight flicks on.

He's there, holding it up. It casts a soft beam in the shape of a smile.

I lift my candle.

He sits by the window with it, just holding the light between us.

We stay like that for almost an hour, two shadows in the dark, watching the storm unravel.

I press my hand to the glass.

After a moment, he does the same.

Our palms don't touch, not really. But I feel something pass through the pane.

A stillness. A warmth.

A maybe.

The first note appears two days later.

In plain white paper, folded and taped to my door. The handwriting inside is neat, slender, and no-nonsense.

"Hi. I'm Winston. I'm sorry if it's weird, but I asked the security guard which unit had the girl who always reads in the window. I'd like to know your name. If that's okay."

"PS: You have excellent taste in instant noodles."

I laugh so loudly I scare my neighbor's cat. It gives me a judgmental stare before padding off down the corridor.

I write back.

"Hi Winston. I'm Charlene. And yes, it's okay. I've been calling you Window Boy in my head, so this is a huge upgrade."

"PPS: I have excellent taste in many things."

The next day, a new note appears.

"I'm sure you do. Want to prove it? Coffee?"

Our first real, face-to-face conversation doesn't happen until three weeks later.

We meet at the corner café a block away.

He's taller in person. Warm and good-natured, but nervous in a way that makes me feel braver.

His good blue shirt is slightly untucked from his jeans in one corner.

I decide, right then and there, that I like him.

We talk for three hours. About everything. About nothing. It's easy.

He listens like I'm a song he's trying to learn by heart.

When we say goodbye, he doesn't kiss me.

He just gives my hand a quick squeeze and says, "I'll see you at the window."

And I do.

Every day. Every night.

It's like clockwork. A comfort I almost crave like air, something I didn't know I needed until it was right there through the glass.

We fall in love through the window.

With scribbled signs. With matching cups. With watching the same movie and reacting in real time, holding up rating cards we made for each other. Mine has his choice of old laptop cardboard boxes cut into squares; his are colored pink and decorated with fluffy cats in varying moods.

We meet on weekends. We get takeout and hang out at his place.

We take long walks in the neighborhood. Somehow, it always happens right after there's rain, when it feels like something's coming back to life.

In late-night conversations, he tells me things slowly, almost thoughtfully. I learn not to rush the quiet.

He kisses me in the elevator once, just before the doors open for him to step out. I giggle for three floors afterward. My neighbor's cat judges me once more, but I can see the grudging approval now.

One time, after sharing a bucket of fried chicken for dinner, he brushes a strand of hair behind my ear like it's the most natural thing in the world.

It is.

⌒

The day we say *I love you*, it happens at the window.

No theatrics. No music.

Just two people holding up signs at the same time, accidentally, ridiculously in sync.

On white cardboard, his says: *"I think I'm falling for you."*

On a pink A4 with fluffy cats, mine answers: *"I already love you."*

We both start laughing. Then crying. Then laughing again.

Later, he comes over and kisses me like my laughter is a secret he finally knows.

And I think maybe we always knew this was going to happen.

From the very first wave. From the first silence we filled together.

Now, I watch him sleep on my couch. He fell asleep halfway through a movie. His coffee's gone cold on the table. His glasses slide down his nose.

I take a blanket from the closet and tuck it around his long limbs. I take his glasses off and put it carefully on the table.

I kiss him on the lips, then rise slowly.

Even though he's here with me, I press my hand to the window.

Out of habit. Out of gratitude.

I can see it's drizzling.

The apartment across from mine is dark now. It looks still, but not empty. Not really.

It's filled with the silence between two heartbeats.

It's full of memory. Of promise. Of waiting.

Of my love for my Window Boy.

And this time, when I reach for the glass, I feel him put his palm over my knuckles.

His other arm goes around my waist. He presses his lips to my hair.

"Hi," he murmurs.

"Hi," I echo.

He feels warm.

Real. Close enough to hold.

At last.

CHAPTER 3

Wrong Number, Right Love

The first time it happens, I'm still at the office.

It's a little past nine in the evening, and the fluorescent lights hum louder than my own pulse. The rest of the floor is empty, but I'm still here, squinting at spreadsheets for the president of the health services company where I work as his personal assistant.

My phone buzzes.

It's a strange number, one not on my extensive contacts list.

I pick up without thinking. "Yes, hello?"

There's a pause. Then a male voice, low and slightly panicked, says, *"Wait. This isn't Paolo?"*

"No," I answer, frowning at the glowing monitor. "This is Edna."

"Oh. Uh…sorry. Wrong number. Carry on. Goodnight."

He hangs up before I can respond.

I roll my eyes, but something about his voice

lingers—warm, flustered, the sound of someone caught sneaking into the wrong classroom.

❧

The second time, it's past midnight, and I'm at my kitchen counter inhaling leftover *siomai* and instant noodles, debating whether to eat or just go straight to bed.

My phone pings.

It's a text.

Last minute cancellation again.

30 more burpees next session.

I blink at the message. What the actual hell.

I type furiously in response.

Sorry.

Who is this?

The answer comes almost immediately.

Not Paolo?

I stick my tongue out at the screen.

Still not Paolo.

The response pings like lightning.

Then who's suffering my training threats?

I smirk despite myself.

Edna.

A very tired PA with zero intention of doing burpees.

Sorry not sorry.

There's a beat, then another ping.

Hi Edna! I'm Zeke!

Future doctor, part-time gym torturer.

Promise I'm not a stalker.

Just really bad at saving contacts.

Against my better judgment, I laugh. Out loud. At past midnight, alone in my apartment.

It becomes a pattern.

Accidental texts. Wrong calls that somehow don't feel wrong.

One night, he sends me a blurry picture of his anatomy notes, ranting about a professor who thinks students don't need sleep.

"*PA life agrees,*" I reply. "*Sleep is a myth. Caffeine is a food group.*"

"*At least you sit. I'm on my feet 12 hours a day, teaching people who think planking for 15 seconds equals death.*"

"*That IS death,*" I shoot back.

Another night, I complain about my boss adding three new meetings to my schedule after eight in the evening.

"*That should be illegal,*" he replies. "*Tomorrow, skip work. Come train with me. Or just hang out.*"

"*No thanks. My idea of cardio is chasing the president with papers to sign. Knowing you, hanging out will literally mean hanging from something.*"

"*You're killing me, Short Stuff.*"

"*How do you know I'm short?*"

"Because you text like someone who glares up at skyscrapers in Megaworld, just because."

I laugh so hard I nearly choke on stale crackers.

❧

The calls start next. Not accidents this time.

"Can't sleep," he says once, his voice a little husky with exhaustion. *"Thought maybe you couldn't either."*

He's right. I'm at the office again, staring at my boss' overflowing inbox.

"You're crazy," I mutter.

But I don't hang up. Because we both are.

Instead, we talk. About nothing. About everything.

He tells me he grew up with two brothers and endless sun, that his tan is permanent proof of being forced outdoors while everyone else gamed.

I tell him I was the bookish girl whose mother packed whitening lotion into every bag, though it never worked on the shadows under my eyes.

"You work too much," he says one night.

"You flirt too much," I retort.

"That wasn't flirting." His voice drops a notch. *"This is."*

I freeze. The silence crackles. My heart does a strange flip.

I hang up.

But the next night, I answer again.

By week four, I know his exam schedule, his favorite protein shake flavor, and his least favorite exercise (*"mountain climbers are Satan's work"*).

By week five, he knows how many sugars I sneak into my coffee, the fact that I hum 90s pop songs when stressed, and that I keep three different planners because one is never enough.

"Control freak," he teases.

"Muscle freak," I fire back.

He laughs so hard he coughs.

But sometimes it tilts serious.

"You're always tired," he says during one call.

"So are you."

"Yeah, but you're…different tired. You sound like you've forgotten how it feels not to be."

The words lodge in my throat. I change the subject.

Then for one week, there's only silence.

No late-night rants. No accidental pings.

I try not to notice.

I fail.

On Friday night, my phone finally buzzes.

Sorry.

Exams.

Didn't want to bother you.

My chest eases as I type my response.

You should have.

I'm excellent at distractions.

Both ways.

A minute later, the phone rings. His deep chuckle fills the line.

"Okay, I'm all yours. Distract me please."

And I do.

For hours.

It happens on a Monday. Almost Tuesday.

I reach my apartment at nearly midnight after staying in the office until eleven.

My phone buzzes with his fourth call that evening. I haven't picked up the first three.

This time, I swipe to accept.

His voice crackles over the line without his usual opening jokes or jabs.

"Where are you? Are you okay?"

I stare at the screen. "What?"

"Are you okay?" he repeats.

I swallow hard. "Yeah. I was stuck at work finishing a presentation for my boss. He was asked to speak at a convention in Boracay at the last minute. He's traveling in the next few hours."

I hear him exhale slowly over the line. *"Oh. Good. You*

got me worried for a minute there. I must have drank three cans of Red Bull just so I could stay awake."

"What?" I repeat. "Why?"

"*You didn't answer,*" he says. "*Thought maybe something bad happened. I was one energy drink away from stalking your office.*"

I stare at the phone again. It's the last thing I expect him to say, but it warms my empty stomach.

"Something did happen," I answer honestly. "Not bad. Not at all. But I was needed."

"*Needed?*"

"Yeah. There was something important to do—and I did it. That's got to mean something."

He's quiet for a few moments. Then he says, "*You know what I thought, the first time I heard your voice?*"

"What?"

"*That you sounded tired. But underneath it, strong. You were carrying too much, but still carrying it anyway.*"

I blink away the sting in my eyes, throat tight. "That's… accurate."

"*I like accurate,*" he says softly.

We don't talk for nearly half a minute, but I break the silence.

"Zeke? Still there?"

"*Always here for you.*"

I don't know whether to laugh or cry at that.

"You wanna know what I'm carrying?"

"*Hit me. I got all night. I didn't drink all those Red Bulls for nothing.*"

So I tell him.

About my father who had a real family aside from us. About my mother who lost the battle to two lumps in her ovaries shortly after I finished high school.

About my little brother who lives with my elderly grandparents in Bacolod City and goes to college at UNO-R. About my job that helps me carry them all.

And he listens.

⌒

We last nearly two months like this. Voices in the night, names and messages on screens.

Then one evening, he texts.

What if we stopped being just wrong numbers?

Coffee?

My stomach flips.

I should say no. I don't do things like this. My life is schedules, reminders, alarms.

Beyond those…I don't really know.

But my fingers type the answer from my heart before my brain can take over.

Sure.

⌒

He's waiting when I arrive at the all-hours coffee shop down the road from my building.

I recognize him immediately.

The sight of him is a little too much. Lean and tall, shoulders filling out a plain black T-shirt. His arms are ridiculous, roped with muscle, tan skin stretched over veins like a sketch out of a textbook.

His smile is immediate, almost blinding. It's the kind of smile that says he's been saving it for someone in particular.

"Edna?"

His voice is the same one that's lulled me through insomnia, the same laugh that's pulled me from exhaustion. Now it has a face, sharp-featured and sun-warmed, real enough to make me want to run or stay forever.

"Zeke," I breathe.

The moment feels strange and not strange at all.

He grins down at me. "You weren't kidding. Short Stuff."

Heat rushes to my cheeks. I'm just grateful that it's nighttime. "You weren't kidding. Gym Freak."

He buys me an iced latte. We sit. We talk. And it's too easy. His laugh is louder in person, his eyes darker, his presence somehow more magnetic than I'd prepared for.

I'm acutely aware of my chubby arms, my pale skin, the faint creases in my blouse. Next to him—tan, ripped, glowing with health—I feel like a before-photo from a makeover that never happened.

Halfway through, I excuse myself to the bathroom, stare into the mirror, and whisper, "Don't get carried away, Edna. This isn't for you."

When I come back, his smile falters. "You okay?"

"I just... I don't know what you're expecting," I say,

words tumbling before I can stop them. "You're…" I gesture helplessly at his broad chest, his impossible shoulders. "And I'm…"

I take a deep breath. Then I say it.

"This could all just be what it really was."

He regards me curiously, one eyebrow slightly lifted. "And what's that?"

"A mistake."

His chair scrapes back. He's in front of me before I can retreat, towering, his presence like heat and shadow.

"Don't," he says softly. "Don't compare us like that. I didn't spend months falling asleep to your voice because of what you look like. I came here for you."

I blink up at him, stomach clenching with nerves. "But what if this screws it up?"

His jaw tightens. Then he crouches down in front of me and leans over, close enough that his breath brushes my cheek. "Then let me screw it up properly."

And he kisses me.

It's not a tentative brush. It's not even a polite or platonic peck.

It's a collision.

It's hot and urgent, months of exchanged emojis and midnight laughter pouring into one desperate press of lips.

He tastes like coffee and heat and something I don't want to let go of. His mouth moves against mine with a confidence that makes my knees buckle, his hand sliding to the small of my back to steady me, dragging me closer until I'm flush against him.

I gasp, and he swallows the sound, deepening the kiss until the world lurches. My hands clutch his shirt, fingers bunching fabric over muscle that feels like steel under my palms.

When he finally pulls back, both of us are breathing like we've run a marathon. His lips still hover at my jaw as he rasps, "Still think this is a mistake?"

I shake my head, dizzy and overwhelmed.

"Best wrong number of my life."

Two nights later, I stumble out of the office at almost ten in the evening, shoes pinching, tote heavy with paperwork for an upcoming board meeting.

My phone buzzes.

It's a message from Zeke.

Look up.

I frown, then obey.

And there he is.

He's perched on a low wall separating our building from the one next to it. He's still in his gym tee, arms crossed, watching me like I'm the only thing worth seeing.

Before I can scold him for waiting so late and not telling me he's there, he jumps down and strides over.

Then he scoops me up like I weigh nothing, lifting me clean off the ground.

"Zeke!" I squeak, kicking uselessly, my arms flying around his neck.

"Relax, Short Stuff," he murmurs against my ear. "I'll always be here to help you carry it all. Starting with you."

I bury my face in his shoulder, laughing breathlessly as he spins me once, the city blurring around us.

For the first time in forever, I don't feel tired.

I feel alive.

All because of a mistake that led me to where I'm meant to be.

CHAPTER 4

Bookshop Hours

IT STARTS AT THE POETRY SECTION.

He's always there before me, standing with his head slightly inclined, wavy black hair unruly, glasses sliding down his nose. He's always wearing a light-colored shirt over dark jeans and impeccably polished brown boots.

Sometimes he's flipping through Neruda, other times it's a thin chapbook I've never heard of. Other times he's at the non-fiction shelves frowning at autobiographies.

I pretend not to notice. I drift aimlessly, fingers grazing spines, heart hammering like I'm sixteen again.

I always end up picking something by Khalil Gibran. Other times I just go to women's fiction and pick Judith Krantz because I don't have the energy to get overly emotional.

Sometimes he steps aside to let me pass. Sometimes I do the same for him. We never say a word.

It's easier that way.

The shop itself is strange. It's a 24-hour secondhand bookstore and café in the middle of a city that never sleeps. It smells like old paper, burnt espresso, and rain from the sidewalk. The kind of place that feels like it doesn't belong in this timeline.

I come here because I don't know where else to go after work. My job drains me, my apartment feels empty, and here at least, there are books and people who don't ask questions.

And him.

Always him.

⤫

It becomes a pattern.

I see him tucked into the corner table with his laptop when he's not browsing.

And he sees me. I know he does.

Sometimes he leaves a scrap of paper on his table with a short verse written on the back.

I find the first one particularly gray and damp Thursday afternoon.

"Every day you play with the light of the universe."

For some reason, it makes me smile.

Three days later, I see another. This time, the words are from Gibran.

"Your pain is the breaking of the shell that encloses your understanding."

When I reach my apartment that night, I sit on the couch for an hour, crying at first, then laughing.

Then I cry again until my tears are all gone.

It's insane, but it's also the most alive I've felt in months.

The night it happens, the storm rolls in sudden and loud.

Thunder rattles the windows. Rain slams against the roof.

And then darkness.

The power cuts out, plunging the shop into shadow.

Gasps ripple from the handful of customers still inside. The barista and cashier fumble for emergency lamps and candles, muttering apologies.

I freeze near the poetry shelf, still clutching a worn copy of D.H. Lawrence's *Birds, Beasts and Flowers*, my phone torch shaky in my hand.

And then he's there.

"Hey," he says softly, his voice warmer than I imagined. "You okay?"

I nod, a little too fast. "Yeah. Just…wasn't expecting that."

He smiles, the kind that glows even in the dim light. "Guess we're stuck until the storm passes. Or at least until the power comes back on."

I nod again, my pulse kicking hard.

His smile grows wider. "Unless you wanna brave the rain and the wind—and the dark? In which case, chivalry dictates I should escort you to safety."

A smile blooms across my face, no matter how hard I try to play it cool.

"You sound like you belong in the wrong century," I say.

He shakes his head. "Chivalry is never out of century or style." He extends a hand. "Well? Into the storm? Through the dark?"

I giggle, shaking my own head in response.

"No," I answer, taking his hand. "To the corner table."

He leads me to his usual table, and pulls out a chair for me.

After I take my seat, he disappears into the shadows of the darkened shop and returns minutes later with two glasses of iced chocolate topped with cream and real chocolate shavings.

"Someone ran off before they got their order," he says simply, as he puts the first glass before me. "Didn't want these two perfectly untouched servings of iced choco to go to waste."

"Very smart," I intone. "How much do I owe you?"

He takes the seat across from mine. "Nothing. It's on the house."

I eye him closely. "Or on you?"

He tilts his head with a broad grin, his teeth gleaming white in the dim light. "You could say both."

That explains a lot. The constant presence. The way he moves around the shop with such quiet, comfortable familiarity.

"Well, thanks," I say, feeling a little warm at the way his

eyes can't seem to look away from me, now that we're seated face to face.

"I've seen you here before," he says, taking a sip of his drink.

I laugh nervously. "Yeah. I've…seen you too."

"Poetry shelf, right?" His eyes crinkle. "You almost always reach for the same side. Gibran fan. Sometimes D.H. Lawrence."

I flush. "And you always pretend not to notice."

"Guilty." He leans in. "I'm Carlo."

"Alice." My name feels fragile, new as I say it to someone else.

He grins. "It suits you."

We talk through the storm, through the dark.

About books, about music, about why I haunt this place like a restless ghost. I admit I come here because I don't know where else to go when I can't stand my own walls, after a long dreary day of evaluating health insurance claims.

He tells me he used to work abroad, teaching technical English in the vast oil fields of Saudi Arabia. But something about the written word brought him home and made him start his own printing press, all digital, able to cater to more modest runs from smaller publishers. He'd bought this bookstore from a National Artist of Literature as a passion project a few years ago, then added an all-hours coffee shop as a nod to their family business in Iloilo.

Somehow it's easy. Too easy. It's as if we've been in a conversation for months without saying a word until now.

The candles flicker. The storm softens. But his eyes never leave mine.

❧

When the power finally comes back on, most people clap in relief. But I feel disappointment sink in my chest.

"Looks like we're free," I murmur.

"Yeah." He hesitates, then says, "Or…we could stay a little longer."

Something in his voice makes my breath catch.

I nod. "Yeah. Let's."

He takes my hand and we drift back to the poetry shelf, side by side this time. He pulls out a thin volume, flips to a page, and hands it to me.

Read this, his eyes seem to say.

I read aloud, my voice trembling a little, but steady enough to form the words.

"I want to do with you what spring does with the cherry trees."

Silence.

His hand brushes mine tentatively, asking.

I don't pull away.

Then he leans closer, carefully, giving me time to change my mind.

I don't.

The kiss is soft at first, a promise more than a question. But when I tilt my head up toward his and press my lips back harder, it deepens.

It becomes warm and insistent, then hot and dizzying. His hand cradles my jaw, the other finds its way to my waist. My arms reach up, anchoring myself to his shoulders.

I forget the storm. I forget the silence of my apartment, the ache of empty nights. I forget the grayness of days and tasks that never really end.

There's only the taste of him, the heat of him, the impossible, undeniable rightness of this moment.

When we break apart, both of us are breathing hard. He puts his arms around me and draws me close.

"I've been waiting," he admits, voice raw. "Alice in my bookshop."

I giggle, then gasp as he kisses me again.

"Me, too," I murmur. "Me too."

⌒⊙

We leave together just before dawn.

The streets glisten from the storm, puddles glowing under streetlamps. The air smells of wet asphalt and earth, the city quieter than I've ever known it.

Carlo drives me to my block in a neat black sedan, then insists on escorting me to my apartment. We walk close enough that our arms brush now and then. Neither of us rushes.

At my door on the second floor, he hesitates.

"So…" His voice is careful, almost shy. "This is you?"

I nod. "Yeah. End of the line. Consider your knightly duties fulfilled, sir."

He smiles, but it wavers.

And I understand why.

He doesn't want the night to end either.

Something inside me clicks with certainty, gentle and tender.

I look at him, really look, at his hair damp from rain, the warmth in his eyes that I've been waiting months to touch, the gentle hands that have written and shared poetry with me.

"You could come in," I say softly. "If you want."

His breath catches.

A pause, then he nods, a slow smile lighting up his face. "Yeah. I want."

My hands shake a little unlocking the door, but when it swings open, the world feels warmer and steadier.

And when I step into my four walls, it somehow feels new this time.

He steps inside with me.

I close the door behind him.

And whatever happens after belongs only to us.

The sunlight through my curtains feels different.

Softer. Less lonely.

Carlo is still here, clad only in shorts and barefoot in my kitchen, chucking quietly as he gets my old coffee machine to work.

"Coffee is in your genes," I say softly.

He glances up when he catches me watching him from the narrow doorway. "Hey."

"Hey." My voice is rough with sleep, but my smile feels easy.

He crosses the room and takes me into his arms without hesitation, pressing a warm, wet kiss to my mouth. I squeal when his tongue sneaks in.

I punch him lightly on the chest when he draws back to pull out a chair at the tiny kitchen table. As soon as I'm seated, he puts a steaming mug of coffee in front of me, followed by a plate of perfectly made twin sunny side-up.

"So…I'll see you tonight?"

I laugh, the sound bubbling out of me before I can stop it.

"Yeah," I say. "I'll see you at the shop."

He shakes his head as he takes the seat next to mine.

"No. I'm picking you up as soon as you finish work. We're going to look for new places to haunt together."

Then he leans over to kiss me again.

And I kiss him right back.

I don't even get to touch the eggs or the coffee, because I end up in his arms, laughing as he scoops me up and carries me back to bed.

And just like that, it isn't just about the bookshop or the walls around me anymore.

It's about everything after.

It's about everything beyond.

CHAPTER 5
Chained to You

IT'S NOT MUCH, BUT I KNOW SHE'LL NOTICE.

She always does.

I set the small box of cookies on her desk before heading to my office. It's a routine by now. Whenever I'm sent offsite, I bring something back for Trina. Local delicacies, small tokens.

Two months in Pampanga felt longer than that. Endless rounds of audits, fourteen-hour days, numbers blurring until even the ledgers seemed to complain. I'm glad to be back, even if my desk at Assassins' Block looks exactly as I left it. Two computer screens lit, bare walls save for a few certificates and photos, the familiar scent of strong black coffee filling the room.

I don't hear her approach until she's standing in the doorway.

Trina's smiling like she already knew I'd be here. She crosses the floor with that familiar energy that always cuts through the monotony of spreadsheets.

I get to my feet instantly, relief washing over me, and pull her into a hug.

"Welcome back, VAT," she teases, arms looping around me. That nickname, born of my initials and her quick wit years ago, stuck harder than any title the firm ever gave me.

Her presence is grounding, the kind of comfort that lingers. She smells faintly of something floral, light, as her voice warms the space between us.

"You look so brown," she says, half-mocking. "Eaten one too many plates of *sisig*?"

I laugh, brushing a quick kiss against her cheek. "Jealous much? It's good to be back. How have you been, Trina?"

She gives me a peck in return, as casual as ever, though I can tell she means it. "It's been busy around here. I had no one to complain to these past few months, though. You missed a lot."

I study her as I sit back down. Same quick eyes, same restless smile. I've always admired how she can make even complaints sound like sunshine.

"I'm sure I did," I reply. "With you around, I'll catch up in no time."

She claims the chair across from me, folding one leg under her. "How are you? Did anything exciting happen in Pampanga?"

"If you call spending fourteen hours a day with ledgers exciting, then yes—very exciting. I had the time of my life."

"You're no fun, Vince."

"You're welcome to all the fun, Trina." I can't help but smile indulgently. She deserves better than my tired jokes, but it's all I've got. "I'll stick to my balance sheets. I don't think I've got energy for much else."

She frowns, pouts even, like I've disappointed her yet again.

Then she drops it casually, almost playfully.

"Well, you'd better have enough energy to dance at my wedding, at least."

My hand freezes on the mouse. The words land heavier than I expect, and I feel one eyebrow shoot up before I can stop it.

"Abella asked?"

"Not yet," she says quickly. "Soon. Maybe this weekend. We're having dinner on Saturday night. Five-star hotel, the works. He's pulling out all the stops."

I lean back in my chair, letting the information settle. My chest tightens for a second, but I force it away with practiced calm.

"Well," I say lightly, "in exchange for the cookies, I'm claiming first dibs on the happy news."

She rolls her eyes as she stands, already halfway out the door. "I've got to go for our team meeting. I never knew those cookies had a price, though."

I switch into Presentation Mode, the voice I save for clients, deliberately serious. "Miss David, you have worked for this firm your entire professional life. You should know by now that everything has a price."

She laughs as she leaves, and for a moment, my office feels less empty.

It's Saturday.

I pluck a dart off the coffee table, aim, and let it fly. The tip buries itself into the square of paper I pinned to the reminders board. Right through today's date on the desk calendar. Exactly where I wanted it.

Today.

Saturday.

My body doesn't know rest days. I'm up at five sharp, same as always. I lace up my shoes, step outside, and run my usual loop past Pasay City Sports Complex.

Asphalt, sweat, breath. A steady ritual.

I come back, shower, cook oatmeal and eggs, drink black coffee. Routine.

And tonight, I need to get out.

The text came in at eleven last night.

R1: 100% Stock Engine & Chassis

R2: Stock 4Stroke

R3: Stock 4Stroke Automatic

R4: Open to All Brands & Models

Track: Legal confirm 8PM Sat 22/4

Entry: TBC msg 9PM Sat 22/4

I know what that means. Another run.

I've been in the underground drag circuit for years now. Out there, I'm not Vincent Tugade, auditor. I'm the King of Chains—the black Dodge, the leather jacket, the insignia my father drew once on a scrap of paper. He never saw it on a hood, but I made sure I would.

Cars were the language between us. My father worked for the government, but weekends belonged to the garage. Engines, gears, grease. He passed the passion to me before a drunk driver took both my parents away in one night.

I was eighteen. Old enough to drive, young enough to think I could outpace grief. I dragged my sister Veronica, ten years old and shell-shocked, out of the province and into Manila, where our aunt took us in. I worked as her errand boy, fixed her old ToyoPet, and balanced the books at the school cafeteria when no one else could.

Numbers came easy. Engines came easier. By the time I started college, I was already sneaking into races with my aunt's patched-up ride.

Now I've got my own cars. A condo. A degree. A life split down the middle; audits by day, races by night. Veronica went back to the province after our aunt passed away two years ago. She's a nurse now.

I'm alone. And I like it that way.

Second cup of coffee in hand, I'm about to head down to the basement to check the Dodge when my phone rings. The name flashing on the screen makes me pause.

Trina.

Of all people.

I pick up.

"Hello, Trina." I try to sound neutral, but I already feel the balance of my day tilt. "How are you?"

What I get back isn't her usual firecracker tone. No jokes. No bright chatter. Just a subdued voice that barely sounds like her.

"Hi, Vince. I'm so sorry for bothering you. Did I call at a bad time?"

I frown. "No, not at all. Everything okay?"

"You got a minute to talk? Please?"

I drop onto the couch, my mug balanced on my knee. "Sure. Anything for you. What's up?"

There's a pause. Then she says the name.

"James."

Abella. The prick.

I bite back the instinct to comment. He's her boyfriend. Her problem. Not mine.

Still, my fists clench just thinking of him. Shiny on the outside, hollow underneath. Like racers who blow their cash on paint jobs and forget their oil changes. All flash, no substance.

"Has he done something? Are you okay?"

"Nothing like that. I'm fine." But her voice doesn't sound fine.

I steady myself. The same way when Veronica called about some boy breaking her heart. "Okay then. Just let me know if there's anything I can do."

Maybe, just maybe, run Abella over. She could pick which car I'd use.

"Vince… what happens if I don't want to?"

My brow furrows. "Don't want to what?"

"You know. The S-word."

I almost spit my coffee. I set the mug down carefully, like the damn thing might explode.

"Wasn't he going to propose tonight?" I manage. "Five-star hotel, all that?"

"He wants to take our relationship further. If he does ask me to marry him, and I say yes, he might want a…"

"Test drive?" The words leave before I can stop them.

"Yes." The answer is flat, humorless.

The silence stretches. My head pounds with all the things I could say but don't.

"What do you want to do, Trina?" I ask instead.

A sharp breath comes through. *"I don't know. That's why I called you. To ask a man how he would feel if his fiancée refused to…you know."*

Dangerous ground. I'm no spokesman for that bastard.

"Has he asked you before?" I swallow hard. "Have you… done it with him before?"

My face burns. I crunch numbers for a living, not give relationship and intimacy advice.

"No. Never. I tried, Vince. I can't…"

Her words break off.

I keep my voice even. Gentle. "Then don't give in, if you don't want to."

"Wouldn't that frustrate him? Make him angry? Turn him off?"

"If he really loves you and wants to marry you, he should damn well be willing to wait."

There's a pause, then she asks softly, *"Would you wait, Vince? If you were in his place?"*

"You know me better than that," I say before I can stop myself. "I'd never put you in that position. That's not love, Trina. Not even close."

The quiet static on the line presses down on me. This isn't supposed to be about me. Not in the fucking least.

She exhales slowly. *"I never thought of it that way. When James first became my boyfriend, I was so happy. Everyone kept telling me how lucky I was."*

Not everyone.

"He's so handsome," she continues. *"So dreamy. A famous model. All that. I thought I had to keep him happy, to keep him."*

"Are you happy now?" I ask.

She doesn't hesitate. *"To be honest, it's hard to be happy when your relationship is like a ticking time bomb. Lately, all I can think about is what happens when he asks. What if I can't give him what he wants? What if I make the wrong decision? What if he leaves me?"*

"It sounds like you're thinking too much about him, and not enough about yourself," I say. "What if you think about what would make you happy?"

"Me? I don't know."

"Once you figure it out," I say, "I get first dibs. I'll even buy you those nasty sweet cookies from Greenbelt you like."

A small giggle escapes her, and I let out a slow breath to relieve the clenched sensation in my chest.

"Yeah, those," she says.

"Think about what makes you happy, Trina. Make your decisions based on that. Not on what makes someone else happy, especially at your expense."

"Thanks, VAT," she murmurs. *"You're the best, you know that?"*

"Don't tell anyone. My services are exclusive."

"To me?" There's the playful lilt again, thank God.

"Always have been."

"See you Monday, Vince. Sorry for bothering you."

"It's okay. You can bother me anytime."

She thanks me again and hangs up.

I plug the phone into its charger and lift my mug for a sip. The coffee's cold now. It tastes flat, bitter. The way I feel, thinking about her.

Thinking about Abella.

Thinking about Trina, again.

Six years ago, she was the first face I saw at the firm. Pre-interview, clipboard in hand, voice quick and bright. I thought she was the most breathtaking woman I'd ever met.

I still do.

She was chaos, chatter, energy—everything I wasn't. And somehow, she made space for herself in my life, never letting me shut her out the way I shut out everyone else.

Numbers obey rules. Engines obey design. Trina breaks both.

And I let her.

I tell her to think about her happiness, but when it comes to mine? I don't. I can't. Not when she's with him.

I know already how this ends. Either I see a ring on her finger, or I watch her walk down the aisle.

Either or both will tear me apart, but I'll take it. Quietly. Alone.

Held back by chains of my own making.

It's time.

Even after all these years, the anticipation still grips me the same way. The faster heartbeat, the damp palms, the knot low in my stomach. Soon the nerves will fade into focus.

And when the flag drops—adrenaline, pure and consuming.

In the dim garage beneath my building, Eskeleto waits. My Dodge, my weapon, my escape. I run my hands along her frame, checking every inch. She's perfect, as always. I whisper to her the way other men pray.

"Let's do this, old friend."

Her hood bears my mark: the chain, the skull, and the pocket watch. Life, death, and time, all bound together.

Time. Always time.

What I wouldn't give for more of it. More time with Trina before she vanishes into a life that doesn't include me. Before Abella claims her like a prize on his arm.

I sigh.

I'm fucked. And I know it. The only way I deal is the way I always deal.

I drive.

I slide into the seat, grip the wheel, twist the ignition. Eskeleto roars awake, the sound filling my chest, drowning everything else out. Across from us sits T-Baby, my gray Toyota.

The commuter, the errand girl, the lovesick fool of a car. I give her one last look as if I'm saying goodbye to the softer side of me, the side that wonders about different directions and safer destinations.

Then I floor it.

The city lights blur, neon and sodium glow streaking past as I cut through Manila's veins. By the time I reach the Bay, the track is alive.

Engines growling, voices jeering, the sea's salt bite mixing with gasoline and rubber. The underground is church, and I am its high priest.

I park at my spot, the neon skull marking the ground. People close in, calling out, hands reaching for mine.

"King of Chains!" they shout, as soon as they see me step out of the car.

The title follows me everywhere.

"Good luck, boss!" one kid stammers, his palm clammy in mine.

"Thanks," I tell him, putting on the smile they expect. "Good luck to all of you."

The mask slides into place. Confidence.

I'm supposed to be invincible.

Untouchable.

"Vincent! Over here!"

The voices of women cut through the din. They're draped over polished cars like goddesses of drift. Eyes lined dark, lips painted red, bodies wrapped in what could only be dark leather. Alena, Florence, the usual suspects. They throw me glances, their eyes and words filled with promises and invitations.

"Celebrate with us later," Alena purrs, tracing her nails along her bulletproof black Volvo's hood.

"Sorry, beautiful. Not tonight. Got to travel tomorrow," I deflect politely.

Florence smirks, ruffling my hair. "Always so focused. That's why you're the best."

I grin for them, say I'll make it up next time. All lies.

Tonight, I couldn't care less. My heart's too busy being somewhere else. With someone else.

Trina.

Her name hums in me, an engine I could never switch off.

By the time I'm at the line, two cars flank me. I don't see them. I don't even hear them. My world shrinks to the wheel in my hands, the machine vibrating under my feet.

The marshal lifts the flag. It's a beauty queen this time, with long legs and a body-hugging red dress, beaming with a perfect smile.

The crowd howls. None of it touches me.

"GO!"

I launch. The world fractures into light and speed,

adrenaline clawing through my veins. Corners blur. Straights vanish. My car and I are one, knife and hand, cutting through the dark.

I reach the finish line before I realize it. The others vanish in my rearview.

It's victory, but I don't feel anything.

The crowd swarms me. I hear cheers, receive handshakes and claps on the back. Kisses from red lips brush against my cheek. I give them what they want, but the thrill's not there.

The win feels like another audit wrapped up, clean and cold. Done, signed, and filed away.

Phil, one of the racers, clasps my shoulder. "Nice win, King of Chains."

"Thanks, man," I reply, forcing a smile.

And then it's over. The crowd dissolves into after-parties, laughter spilling into the night. I climb back into Eskeleto, the silence pressing close.

Rain starts as I cut through the Bay Area, sheets blurring the city into dark watercolor smears.

I should feel free. Instead, I feel chained. No matter how fast I go, I can't outdrive what's in my head.

Trina.

Always her.

I turn a corner—and slam the brakes. Tires shriek. My chest slams the belt.

What the actual fuck.

Because she's there.

In the middle of the rain-slick road, drenched, standing in my headlights.

My mind scrambles for sense.

A trick? A mirage?

Maybe I'm losing it.

No. I'd know her anywhere.

I kill the engine, push the door open, and step into the downpour.

Only one way to know if she's real.

The headlights slice the downpour into strobe-lit stripes.

And there she is, frozen in the beam like a startled animal.

"Trina? What the fuck are you doing here?"

Her eyes squint against the glare. She looks me up and down like she's seeing a ghost in leather and spiky hair.

"Vincent?"

I slog toward her, water pooling in my boots, adrenaline tapering into something more pronounced in my chest.

"Have you lost your goddamn mind, Trina? You shouldn't be out on the road like this."

"Vincent?" she says again, as if the name might change the picture she's seeing. "What are you doing here? Why do you look like that?"

"We have to get you off the street." I hold out a hand. "Come on."

She doesn't take it. Her face has that dazed, post-impact distance. Too much night. Too much everything.

"Get in the car, Trina. Please."

She backs away. "Just go, okay? Leave me alone."

"What the hell are you even doing out here?" I step closer and catch her forearm. "I'm taking you home, okay? Please get in the car and we can talk about it."

I try for the familiar smile she knows. The patient, indulgent one. It doesn't come easy tonight.

"I don't think—"

I move a hand to the small of her back and guide her toward the passenger side. She yields, tired more than willing, and I slide her into the seat. I circle to the driver's side, close us in from the rain, and shrug off my jacket. Underneath, just the black sleeveless shirt. I hand her the jacket.

"Stay warm. I'll kill the A/C."

"Thanks," she says, her voice small.

"You're welcome." I flick switches, adjust the vents. Eskeleto hums back to life. My forearms drip, my tattoos drenched in water and light. I catch her eyes on them and keep mine on the dash.

She buckles in when I do. The leather creaks. The cabin smells like rain and gasoline and her perfume.

We pull out smoothly. I keep the car as steady as I could.

"Vince, I…" She stares at her hands. "I'm sorry."

"For what?"

"For all the trouble. One thing after another went

downhill. Before I knew it, I was out of there like my ass was on fire."

I shake my head, eyes on the road. "In a way, it's good I was the one you ran into. These brakes hold up even when they're wet."

She doesn't say anything. I let the silence sit. The wipers thud steadily.

She glances around the cabin, seeing what she didn't know about me. The skull-and-chain insignia stitched into the seats, the reinforced windshield, the control panel a mad scientist's array of gauges and toggles.

The racer's life I never shared.

"If I'd known you were at the hotel, I would have picked you up," I say. "You should have called me."

"I dragged you through the pathetic story of my relationship this morning," she murmurs. "I couldn't do that to you twice. Besides, I never thought you'd be here, at this time. Like that." She gestures at all of me.

"Like what?"

"Different. Dangerous. You know, someone capable of running James over."

A corner of my mouth lifts. "Whoever said I wasn't? All you have to do is ask."

She breathes out slowly. "That sounds very tempting right now."

"If you really want to do a number on Abella, we can turn back and get him," I say, not joking as much as I should be. "Track by the bay's probably closed, but I can get us in.

I've raced there since they poured the first concrete after the mall opened."

Her gaze drops to the jacket in her lap. A small smile ghosts her mouth. "Thanks for the generous and potentially criminal offer, but I'll pass."

We fall into quiet. I thread us through Saturday-night traffic, cut down side streets only locals use, keeping my speed respectful in the rain.

Her shoulders loosen by degrees. Her death grip on the seatbelt begins to ease.

"You still stay at the tower?" I ask.

"Yes. I'm surprised you remember."

"We'll be there soon. I'll take the shortcut by the hospital. Less late-night congestion."

"You're the best, VAT," she says softly. "Thanks for putting up with my crap."

I don't answer that. A minute later, I rest a hand on her shoulder when I stop at a red light. "It's not crap. I'm sorry this happened. You deserve to be happy."

She pulls the jacket tighter. "At least James had the guts to call it off himself. I suppose he needed something I couldn't give. We both wanted different things. I stressed about it for nothing."

"Not nothing." I keep my tone even. "Whatever you two had meant more to you than it did to him."

Rain blurs the city into streaks of light. She watches it, voice distant. "He met someone in Bali months back. They kept in touch. He said she wasn't…cold. Or walled off. His words."

"Sounds like he thinks you're a high-security vault," I say. "One he doesn't have the access code to. Poor bastard."

She glances over. "I never thought you'd feel sorry for him. You hate his guts."

"Am I that obvious?"

"Kind of. Especially since you offered to run him over."

"That prick doesn't know what he's missing," I say, and I don't leave room for debate.

Minutes later, I pull up in front of her building. I take an open slot at the curb, kill the engine, and swing out. The rain has backed off to a fine spray. I open her door and offer a hand. She steps out carefully. The foyer lights bleach the night off us.

"Thank you, Vince." She slips out of my jacket and hands it back. "For everything."

"You're welcome." I take the jacket. "You okay? Need anything? I can run to the pharmacy, get you some food, or whatever."

"I'm fine. Thanks." Her eyes run over my face like she's trying to reconcile two versions of me. Same man, just in a different light. A different night.

I step closer and slide an arm around her shoulders, then I press a quick kiss to her cheek. It's the same familiar, practiced act, but it hits somewhere unexpected.

"Rest up, Trina. Call me tomorrow if you need anything, okay?"

She doesn't let me step back all the way. Her fingers curl around my forearms, skin on ink.

"Would you like to come up for some coffee?" she asks. Her voice is a touch higher, sounding like she's surprised by the question too.

I hesitate. The predictable version of me would say no. The version in leather is colder, more reckless, but he still knows the rules he lives by.

And yet there's the tug. The chain I made for myself.

"Sure," I say.

❧

What the fuck are you doing, Tugade?

I shadow her out of the elevator, heart pounding louder than it should.

She limps a little, dragging her feet, when we walk down the corridor of the seventh floor. I should help her, but touching her again doesn't sound smart. Not after downstairs. That hug, that kiss on the cheek…they weren't like the others before.

This time, they feel too close for the comfort I'm used to.

She keeps sneaking glances at me, wide-eyed, like she's seeing me for the first time. I know those looks. I've given them to her a thousand times when she wasn't looking. Since the day she walked out to the firm lobby and called my name for the pre-interview.

I've kept it buried. All of it.

For friendship's safe. For the survival of that friendship. If she knew the truth, she'd be gone before I could blink—ass on fire, leaving nothing behind but ashes.

But I can't lose her. Not her trust, not her presence, not her.

She's freshly single. Emotionally raw. This is the worst time to let myself think I might have a chance. I'd rather be flattened by another racer than risk it.

She stops at 704. "Home sweet home. Can you help me, Vince?"

I snap out of it.

She's holding out her keys. "The gold one, please."

I take the bunch too fast, and bend to the lock. Her weight leans into my arm, soft and sudden. Her wet dress clings, curves inches from my face. My throat goes tight.

"I'm so tired, Vince," she sighs. "I think I spent next month's salary shopping this afternoon for an outfit I completely ruined."

Ruined? Nothing about her dress is ruined. It's lethal.

I wrench my eyes away, thank every higher power when the lock clicks open.

Coffee, I tell myself. *Coffee and out.*

She holds on to my arm as we go inside, hobbling but smiling faintly, pointing out switches. I steer her to the couch and finally let go. She sinks into the cushions, then peels off her shoes and rubs her ankles.

"Major ouch," she mutters.

I step back, already half-turned for the door. "I think I'll call it a night. I'd better go."

True to form, she bounces up, barefoot. "What are you talking about? Sit. I'll get you coffee. Premium Arabica. I'll even give you the rest of the beans."

I swallow hard, then nod. I drop onto the couch, leaving my jacket draped over a chair. "Sorry about the wet clothes."

"I did the same thing to your car. Call it even."

She disappears behind a curtain. The living room's bright. It's white, yellow, and orange, neat as a spreadsheet but warm. Very her.

Her head pops out a minute later. "Vince? Come join me in the kitchen. I put on some croissants too."

"That would be great."

The kitchen's compact, if not cozy. Yellow tiles, small window, and a wooden table with two seats. She sets coffee and croissants on the table, then gestures to a chair. I sit.

"Thanks for looking out for me tonight," she says quietly. "Goodness knows I have no business troubling you. I honestly thought this morning was the end of it."

The coffee scalds my tongue. "Is that how you think of yourself, Trina? Trouble?"

She flinches a little, damp dress clinging as she fidgets. I try not to stare. My sanity demands I don't.

"It seems I could never give anyone what they want from me," she says. "I don't know if that's trouble or not."

"It's called making choices," I tell her. "Definitely not trouble."

She rattles off her list. James calling her cold, friends calling her flighty, family calling her empty talk. Each word cuts painfully.

"You agree with any of that?" I ask.

She shakes her head. She explains how she likes her job and dealing with people, why she doesn't want to be part of management and spend her time arguing in meetings. She tells me why she saves money instead of blowing it on vacations with her friends.

She practical and grounded underneath the bright exterior. Everything I've always admired.

"Can't argue with the numbers on that one," I say.

She sighs. "And James…well, tonight sums it up. For the record, he broke it off, but I walked out first."

"There you go. Your choice. If people don't appreciate you, that's their problem."

For the first time tonight, she smiles. For real. It hits like a punch.

"You should think about what you want," I add. "Not what anyone else wants. You deserve to be happy."

If only I could follow my own damn advice.

"This makes me happy," she says softly. "Having you here."

It feels like she drove a knife straight into me. I force a grin, lifting my mug in a toast. "To your happiness, Trina."

Her eyes narrow slightly, cutting into me. "Why do you do this, Vince?"

"Do what?"

"This. Look after me. Without asking for anything in return."

I swallow down a bite of croissant. "We're friends. That's what friends do."

She shakes her head. "I don't know anything about you. Not really. You never told me you had a car like that, or that you race. I don't even know if there's a girl waiting for you somewhere while you babysit me."

I almost laugh. "You know there's no girl. There's no one. And racing…Well, you don't exactly advertise that when you work in a Big Four firm."

Her eyes light up. "Will you take me to a race next time?"

"I'll take you," I say. "Just promise you won't tell anyone at the office. With that dress, you'd fit right in."

"This outfit hasn't been a total waste, then."

"No. Not at all." I check my watch, then stand too quickly. The air's too thin now. "It's late, Trina. I'd better go."

She follows me to the living room, then hands me my jacket and a paper bag of beans. "The coffee, as promised. If you bring it to work Monday, save me some."

"Not a chance." I grin, but it feels weak.

She doesn't roll her eyes. She doesn't even swat my arm like normal.

Instead she looks at me, eyes wide and unguarded, then steps closer. Her arms go around my shoulders. Her face hovers inches from mine.

"Trina?" My voice scrapes low, caught between warning and surrender. "What are you doing?"

Her fingers slide into my hair, tugging me down. "What makes me happy."

And then her mouth is on mine.

Our lips crash together.

The heavy intake of breath I hear and feel is mine.

My body goes taut, every nerve wired too tight. Something falls, crunching under our feet, but the world spins anyway because she's pressed against me.

I should pull away.

I don't.

Her taste floods me—coffee, rain, something sweeter. My arms fold around her, first tentatively, then more tightly.

I kiss her back. Slowly, then harder.

It becomes too urgent. Too dangerous.

But this is everything I ever wanted.

Her hands slide under my shirt, fingers mapping the muscle I spend hours running into shape, and I lose air. I nip at her earlobe, her neck, push the straps of her black dress off her shoulders to bare skin I shouldn't touch. She moans softly, brokenly, and I almost break with her.

"Please don't go," she breathes. "Don't leave me tonight."

Her words gut me. I stop abruptly, my hands frozen in her hair, against her back.

"Trina…" My voice comes out raw and choked. "I'm sorry."

She clutches me tighter, chest heaving. "Sorry? For what?"

I meet her eyes. It feels like drowning. "I can't do this. Not now. You deserve better than this."

"Vince, please…" Her voice shakes, but I hear the need in it.

It mirrors mine.

I cup her face in both hands, forcing myself to breathe evenly. "This isn't me rejecting you. It's about respecting you. Respecting us."

She leans into my palms, trembling. "There's something I need to tell you."

I lace my fingers with hers. "What is it?"

"It has always been you," she says in a rush. "I never knew how to say it. You seemed so unreachable, so…perfect. Every time I was with someone else, I compared them to you. No one ever measured up, VAT. No one."

Her words hit harder than any impact on the track. My chest tightens.

My first instinct isn't to claim her—it's to fix her dress. I smooth the creases, steady my hands, anything to keep from exploding.

Then I pull her into me again, softer this time, and press a kiss to her forehead.

"Goodnight, Trina," I say. "I'll see you Monday."

Her reaction's instant. Fire replaces vulnerability like an explosion.

"Goodnight?" she echoes. "That's all you have to say? After all these years, all this…you never once showed me how much I meant to you!"

I keep my tone gentle. "That's not true."

"Isn't it? If you really cared, you would have been smart enough to see it. To see me."

"Trina, I…" The words don't come. My face feels hollow, drained.

She steps away, bitter in her silence.

I can't let it end there. Not after tonight.

"I don't just care for you." My voice is quiet, but it slices through the air. "I love you."

Her eyes widen, as if the words physically struck her body. She doesn't move.

"Maybe that's why you never saw it," I say, pressing on before I lose the nerve. "Caring is simple. Love isn't. Love is complicated, messy, fucked up. I never figured out how to show it. There's no formula, no numbers to make it clear."

Her eyes shine. They're tears I don't want her to cry.

Especially not because of me.

I can't take it.

I grab my jacket from the floor, the bag of coffee beans still sitting where I dropped them. I don't take it. I can't.

"Goodbye, Trina," I whisper.

Then I walk out before I can destroy us both.

The door shuts behind me, heavy as the weight in my chest.

❧

I feel numb.

My legs carry me down the hall, into the elevator, out of her building, but the rest of me feels locked in ice. I'm breathing raggedly, like I've just run ten kilometers and taken a beating at the finish line.

I slide into Eskeleto, grip the wheel, and drive. Rain sheets across the windshield, the city drowned in shadow. The streets are empty, but inside my head it's chaos.

Why did I leave?

Her voice won't let me go.

"It has always been you."

The words loop in my skull, a chain yanking me backward every time I try to move forward.

Hasn't that been the truth all along? I've always felt her pulling me, even when I tried to bury it, even when I told myself friendship was safer.

"Fuck it all," I mutter, my hands shaking as I squeeze the wheel tighter, afraid I'll lose control of more than just the car.

Why now? Why did I run when she needed me most?

Fear? Cowardice? Or the truth, that admitting how much she means terrifies me more than any finish line ever has?

"Trina," I whisper into the dark, my voice cracking. "I'm sorry, baby. I love you."

The words are out. And with them, clarity crashes over me.

I can't keep running.

Not from her. Not from us.

My foot slams the brake. Eskeleto's tires shriek on wet pavement, the car fishtailing before I wrench her into a hard U-turn.

No more running.

The city blurs past. Lights, water, and asphalt twist around me like a blurry kaleidoscope, but all I see is her face. All I hear is her voice.

All I want is to get back to her.

I push the car harder, pedal to the floor, the roar under me shaking my bones. This isn't like the races. I don't want to win. I just want to finish. I want to lose myself to the one person I could never outrun.

I'm coming back for you, Trina.

I'm out of the car before the engine stops, sprinting through the rain to her building. My fist pounds on her door before I even think to look for a bell.

It swings open almost instantly.

She stands there, eyes red, dress damp, hair undone.

Beautiful. Always beautiful. Even broken, she's the only thing I've ever wanted.

I can't hold back. The words rip out of me.

"I'm sorry for running away, Trina. Maybe I wasn't

ready to hear how you really felt. Maybe I wasn't prepared. But I can't run from you anymore. That's why I'm here."

With a sob, she throws herself against me. Her tears soak through my shirt. My arms wrap around her, locking her to me like I should have done years ago.

"My heart has always belonged to you," I say into her hair. "On the track, they call me the King of Chains. But you…you've always been my Queen."

She lets out a shaky laugh. "Tugade, for someone so smart, you're an idiot."

I chuckle, throat tight. "I promise I won't run anymore. I'm here. I'll always be here."

"Good." She looks up, straight into my eyes, not blinking. "Don't you dare leave me again. And don't even think about leaving me tonight."

Her lips find mine, and I know the truth at last.

This is the only race I was ever meant to lose.

❧

We crash against each other, and the world falls away.

I've wanted this for so long, dreamed of it in the dark corners of my mind, but never let myself believe it could happen. And now…now she's in my arms, kissing me hungrily.

"No one is leaving tonight, Trina," I murmur against her mouth. "Not if this is what you really want."

She nods without hesitation. "This is what I've always wanted. I'm sure."

Relief floods through me. I smile, unable to help it, and gently nudge her backward into the apartment. The door shuts behind us with a quiet click.

I scoop her up before she can protest, then lay her down on the couch and lean over her. I let her feel my weight, my warmth. I hear her heart pounding so fast I can feel it through her chest.

"Vince…" she whispers, her hands sliding to my cheeks, her gaze burning into me.

God. She's so beautiful. Why did I ever think I could survive without this? Without her?

I kiss her again, softer this time. Her lips part beneath mine as her fingers thread through my hair.

I want to drown in her. In her warmth, her scent, the sound of her voice when she whispers my name.

We hold onto each other as if we've both been falling for years and finally found solid ground. Every laugh, every long night in the office, every stolen look—it all led to this.

I pull back just enough to let us both take in air.

"I love you, Trina." The words spill out before I can stop them, raw and shaky, but true in every syllable.

Her eyes turn wet, but they don't look way. "I love you too. I always have. I just didn't know how to tell you."

Her confession unravels me. My arms tighten around her, holding her closer, trying to make up for all the wasted years in a single embrace.

We kiss again, longer and deeper, and in that moment there's nothing else.

No past, no fear, no chains holding us back.

Just us.

☙ ❧

Hours blur. The rain eases, the city quiets, and still we're together.

We make love again and again, then once more. We kiss and laugh and talk in between. We drift from room to room, not caring where we land, only that we're with each other. Sometimes it's urgent, sometimes slow and tender, but always real.

Always us.

By the time the sky lightens, we're tangled in her bed, her hair spilling across my arm, her face pressed to my chest. We fall asleep like this.

I wake to the warmth of her spooned against me, her bare skin soft against mine. My arm is still draped around her waist. For the first time in years, I've overslept. It's past nine, nearly five hours past my usual routine.

But staring down at her peaceful face, her lips still swollen from our kisses, I know this is a new routine I could get used to.

"Good morning," she mumbles, half-asleep, voice sweet and shy.

"Good morning, baby girl." The endearment slips out before I can stop it. It feels right. It feels like us.

She blushes, burying her face in my neck. "Don't look at me like that."

"Like what?"

"Like… that. Like I'm the only person in your universe."

I smile into her hair, because she is. She always has been.

"Trina," I say softly, tilting her chin so she'll meet my eyes. "What happens now?"

She blinks, surprised, but she doesn't say anything.

I push through the nerves anyway. "Would you…be my girlfriend? And someday—hell, I'll say it—I'll have to propose too. Especially since we didn't exactly use…" I trail off awkwardly.

She giggles, the sound like sunlight breaking through the rain. "Yes, Vince. To all of the above."

The knot in my chest loosens, and I kiss her soundly. "I love you."

"I love you, too," she says, eyes sparkling. "Though I still can't believe I fell in love with someone who's secretly an idiot."

I laugh, unashamed, and slip into my best Presentation Mode, my voice mock-formal. "Miss David, allow me to demonstrate what kind of idiot I truly am."

Her laughter fills the room, and with it, I plunge into her waiting arms.

CHAPTER 6
A Dance of Years

THE GYM SMELLS LIKE SWEAT, SUGAR, AND TOO many what-ifs.

My heels ache from my cheap shoes. My makeup is running. There's a rip in the hem of my dress I didn't notice until I sat down after the last slow song.

Everyone's still here, lingering past midnight like they don't want it to end. The party is quiet now. There's less shouting, but more laughter softened by goodbyes. The kind of hush that comes when all the pretending, glitter, and adrenaline fade.

And that's when I see him.

He stands near the exit, half in shadow. He looks like he's waiting for something. Or maybe someone.

He's wearing a blazer that's clearly not his, too big at the shoulders, wrinkled like it's lived three lives. His hair's pure chaos.

But he looks like the most beautiful mess I've ever seen.

He sees me before I say a word.

Of course he does.

He always does.

"Hey," I say softly.

"Hey," he answers.

He gives me a smile. I think I'm the only one who's ever seen it on his face.

We've been us since Grade Two. Since scraped knees and playground alliances and snacks traded at lunch. Since he showed me how to climb trees and get down like a final boss. Since I taught him how to lie convincingly to keep from being suspended for tardiness. Since we started pretending to be characters in our own secret stories.

And somewhere along the way, something stopped being pretend.

But we never talk about the thing we never talk about.

He nods toward me, as if he's trying to find the right words and settling on the simplest. "You looked nice tonight."

I snort, too tired to be flattered. "You mean this disco-ball disaster dress or the frizz halo on my head that breaks the laws of gravity?"

He doesn't find this funny.

"I mean you," he says, scowling.

I forget how to breathe.

Because he's not joking, or even teasing. He's just telling the truth.

I take a step forward, and he doesn't move.

The space between us shrinks, and suddenly everything feels tight—my chest, my throat, the string that's been stretched between us since forever. Tonight it pulls tighter, humming like it might snap or sing.

Someone at the DJ's table plays that last song again.

The slow one. The one we never danced to.

Avril Lavigne's 'I'm With You.'

I glance toward the center of the gym, where couples sway in uneven rhythms.

But I don't move. Neither does he. We just stand here, breathing in the shadow of the quiet we share.

"Do you remember," I murmur, "last summer we got caught in the rain? You gave me your jacket even though you were soaked through and shivering."

He nods. "You never gave it back."

I smile. "Still smells like you."

He smiles back, but it looks like it's breaking something in him to do it. "Is that…a good thing?"

I don't answer. Not with words, at least.

Instead, I reach out, barely. Just enough for my fingers to brush his.

He flinches. It's a ghost of a movement, but I see it.

But slowly, his hand turns, then his fingers hook through mine.

It's not something that screams.

It's a maybe. It's everything and nothing all at once.

It's enough to make my heart ache.

"Aidan," someone calls out into the dark.

We both look.

It's his brother, leaning out the car window, headlights flaring through the gym doors.

"You should go," I say.

And he does what he always does.

He lets go first.

"Goodnight, Raya."

Then he's gone.

We don't speak much after that.

Life does what life always does.

It pulls. It tears. It scatters.

We end up in different cities. In different time zones. With different jobs and different people.

But I still see his name in the corners of my screen.

He likes my photos on socials sometimes. I heart his throwback and nostalgic posts, the ones with song lyrics in the captions. He sends a meme on my birthday that makes me laugh harder than it should. I send him a playlist once, the same one he made me listen to when we danced in the kitchen that one afternoon we were supposed to make spaghetti for our class Christmas party.

We almost call. Almost message. Almost say it.

But we never talk about the thing we never talk about.

Still, when it rains, I reach for that jacket. Still tucked in the back of my closet, still stitched with memories of the boy who waits in the shadows but lets go first.

When I walk through crowded places, I look for messy hair and a blazer that never quite fits.

When I laugh too hard at something, I wonder if he'd find it funny too.

We were never a love story.

Not in the way people write them, or movies make us believe them to be.

We were a feeling. A moment in pockets of time.

A dance that we never had.

But this story stays with me anyway.

⁓

Tonight, there's a wedding at the fanciest resort in town.

They used to be our classmates. They both made it in Dubai and came back home to get married.

There are fairy lights everywhere. Music from the live band floats like glitter and dust in the wind. I'm heading to my car after exchanging greetings and goodbyes when I hear it.

The last song.

That song.

The one from the dance.

I'm With You.

It pulls me back to the ballroom like gravity.

I pause at the doorway, watching the bride and groom slow dance. Other couples are swaying on the dance floor. The singer does a great job at singing in Avril's style.

And my body feels hot and cold at the same time.

That's when I see him.

He's standing by the edge of the crowd, half in shadow. Just watching.

He looks older, broader. Tired in a way that feels achingly familiar.

But it's Aidan.

It's him.

Time stops, or maybe my heart does. Or maybe the world just decided to be kind for once.

Across the room, we lock eyes.

I don't know who moves first.

Maybe it's both of us.

Maybe it's always been both of us, just waiting for the right moment to step forward.

When we meet in the middle of the dance floor, I don't say anything.

He doesn't either.

He just holds out his hand.

This time, I take it.

This time, we don't almost.

This time, we dance all the way through.

And he never lets me go.

CHAPTER 7

Table for Two

I T HAPPENS ON A DAY I WAS SUPPOSED TO BE celebrating.

It's a fucked-up kind of celebration, but still.

Instead, when I give my name to the hostess, she looks panicked.

"I'm so sorry, Mr. Alvarez, but we overbooked. The last available table…well, you'll have to share."

I frown. "Share?"

"Yes. If Miss Moran is willing to, of course." The hostess gestures to the woman in a red dress standing near the podium. I find myself looking into wide, intelligent eyes. She's medium height and shapely, with thick black hair that falls halfway down her back.

The woman stares at me, red lips pursed, clutching her phone like a lifeline.

Or a weapon.

Depends on the angle, really.

I can only blink at her in response. I try to open my mouth, but nothing comes out.

"It's fine," says the woman, not trying to disguise her annoyance. "It's not his fault, is it?"

"No, Miss Moran," says the hostess, lowering her eyes. "And I'm very sorry about this again. There must be something that happened to the booking system that day."

"Are there…other options?" I ask.

"Of course, sir." The hostess looks at the screen in front of her, and then back at me. "I'll have a table waiting for you in an hour and a half, if you're willing to wait."

"It's okay," I say, giving the woman in the red dress a tentative glance. I'm starving, so the possibility of a cellphone being swung at my head seems to be a risk worth taking. "If Miss Moran doesn't mind."

"I don't mind," she says, although the look she's giving me clearly says she does.

The manager comes over to the podium, apologizing profusely to the woman, and then to me. He recognizes me from previous visits and calls me a very valued regular guest. He promises that the meal will be waived and only the drinks will be charged.

"I'll take care of the drinks," I say, looking at the woman again.

She meets my eyes, holds my gaze for a few tense seconds, and finally nods.

"Fine."

⌒

So here we are.

Two strangers at a candlelit table, surrounded by couples

leaning across glasses of wine to whisper secrets. The fact that we're in a five-star hotel makes it weirder than it already is.

Not exactly the Thursday night I had in mind.

For five minutes, we each act like the menus are suddenly the most fascinating works of literature on earth.

Finally, she sighs. "This is ridiculous."

I glance up. "The table-sharing thing or the fact that we're both pretending the other doesn't exist?"

Her lips twitch. "Both."

She closes her menu. "Look, I'll go first. I'm celebrating. In a way, at least. It's the one-year mark. My ex cleaned out my savings. Said he was investing. Turns out 'investing' meant bogus cryptocurrency schemes named after mythical beasts and a side girlfriend in Cebu. I came here to remind myself I can still buy my own damn dinner."

I choke on my water. "Wow. Hard act to follow."

Her eyebrows rise. "Your turn."

I rub the back of my neck. "Caught my fiancée cheating. On my birthday. With my cousin. In my apartment. Today's a year to the day I cleaned out all her stuff from my apartment."

She freezes mid-sip of her mocktail. "No."

"Yup. On the couch. Not really my idea of a surprise party, but there you go."

"Oh my God." She covers her mouth. "I'm so sorry. That's…horrible."

"It's fine." I shrug. "At least I got the cake."

That pulls a laugh out of her. A real one, soft and startled. "You didn't."

"I did. Chocolate mousse. Ate the whole thing while she tried to explain why my cousin was not wearing pants in my living room."

She shakes her head incredulously. "That's the stuff of afternoon TV dramas. Darkly impressive."

"I aim to please."

She lifts her glass in a mock toast. "Very gangsta. Really."

I lift my own glass of red wine. "To gangsta."

"To gangsta," she echoes.

"I'm Gene," I say as I put my glass down. I offer her the bread basket. "Gene Alvarez."

She takes a roll with sesame seeds, giving me a small smile. "Ashley Moran."

The food arrives then. Pasta for her, steak for me. Conversation trickles into something easier.

She tells me she works in finance. I tease her for not seeing through her ex's scam. She rolls her eyes and admits that sometimes a six-pack and perfect hair could be very distracting.

I tell her that I have my own business, third-party industrial laundry and cleaning services, that I inherited from my father, which I keep expanding all over the country. The hotel is one of my first clients when I joined the business at eighteen.

But then I tell her about the tragedy of last year's birthday, including the part where my cousin got into the rideshare wearing only his briefs, to the evil glee of my nosy neighbors in the apartment building.

She shares that her ex started seeing the side piece in Cebu because he felt she "validated" his chosen career as a lifestyle influencer, which meant a lot of abdominal close-ups on his social media reels.

By the time we finish the main course, she's laughing so hard she snorts. And I can't stop smiling, even when my cheeks ache.

To cap off the evening, she orders chocolate mousse for dessert, in my honor.

When the check comes, I pick up the drinks bill as promised. She insists on tipping.

I should leave it at that. A strange one-off dinner with a stranger. I should suggest never doing this again.

But instead, I hear myself say, "Same time next week?"

Her eyes widen. Then, slowly, she nods. "Yeah. Why not?"

One week becomes two. Two become months.

Every Thursday night, we claim the same table. The staff stops giving us curious looks. We stop pretending it's random.

We talk more than I expect. About her job that she doesn't really like. About my business that often demands my attention, even at the strangest hours.

We share movies that feel like comfort food and playlists that carried us through heartbreak. She always orders pasta. I always order steak. At some stage during those weeks, we end up splitting both.

We tell ourselves it's habit. For the sake of convenience. A safe spot to lick our wounds in company.

But every Thursday, I find myself looking forward to her stories—the petty revenge fantasies she never acts on, the quiet dreams she doesn't say outright but honors in anecdotes from her childhood.

She tells me she used to play piano when she was younger. I tell her I used to play basketball before my knee gave out. She admits she still checks her ex's socials sometimes, which got more and more "cringe" over time. I confess I still sleep on the same side of the bed, even though it's empty.

There are silences too. Not awkward, but weighty. I know we're both holding back more than we should.

Eventually, she stops protesting when I pick up the bill.

She doesn't even make a clever quip when I show up one Thursday with a bouquet of roses to "match her dress." She thanks me and presses her nose to the petals, inhaling deeply with a smile on her face.

One night, she comes in late, hair damp from the rain, cheeks flushed. My chest actually aches with relief when I see her walk through the door.

"You thought I wasn't coming?" she teases.

"Maybe," I admit. "I should pick you up next time. Especially when it's raining. The traffic must be hell."

She leans in, eyes bright, voice low. "You'd miss me?"

I don't answer right away. I can't.

But the smile tugging at her mouth tells me she already knows why.

⸙

It's another rainy night when it all changes.

We're almost finished with the main course when she slides her foot against mine under the table. Not by accident.

I don't move away. Neither does she.

By the time dessert arrives, I can't taste anything but her.

I set my fork down, heart pounding. "Ash…this isn't just convenience anymore, is it?"

Her gaze doesn't waver. "No. It's not."

We leave together.

Outside, the street smells like rain. Neon bounces off puddles.

I stop under the awning, breath tight. "Ash…"

But she steps closer, fingertips brushing mine. Her eyes dare me.

So I kiss her.

It starts careful, but the way she melts against me, the way she sighs into my mouth, takes me apart without warning.

It's months of holding back breaking all at once.

When I pull back, she whispers, "Your place?"

My heart slams against my ribs. Then I grin. "Closer than mine's ever been to perfect."

We barely make it through the door.

Her laugh echoes in my living room as I pin her gently against the wall, kissing her deeper, hungrier. Her hands dig into my shirt, tugging me closer, and my palms find the softness of her waist through her red dress, her body fitting perfectly against mine. It's heat and tenderness all tangled up, every Thursday night and every almost spilling over into now.

Then I pause, my lips resting on her temple, giving her the chance to think, to breathe. Or to walk away.

"Tell me to stop, Ash."

She shakes her head. "Don't even think about it, Alvarez."

So I kiss her again, and this time it's not about filling the empty spaces.

It's about beginning something new.

The next morning, I walk into the kitchen and see her in my shirt, sitting at the counter, brows furrowed slightly as she spreads butter on slices of toast.

She looks like she owns the place.

And I know—I won't have it any other way.

"Good morning," she says, smiling when she sees me.

"Good morning," I echo.

Her smile broadens when I bring over two matching

plates from a nearby shelf. I kiss her soundly on the mouth when I set them down before her.

"Table for two, Mr. Alvarez?"

I smile back and kiss her again, certain for the first time in a long time.

"Always."

CHAPTER 8

Letters Across Time

THE DESK CAME WITH THE OLD HOUSE IN Antipolo.

Or maybe the house came with the desk.

It was wedged against the far wall of what looked to be the library on the ground floor, a heavy wooden thing with brass handles. Its surface bore scratches from years of pens and elbows. One drawer stuck stubbornly, as if it resented being opened.

The realtor apologized for the furniture the previous owners had left behind, but I didn't mind. I liked the idea of things carrying history.

It wasn't until I tried to tug the stubborn drawer loose that I found the box.

It was shallow, tucked in a false bottom I almost missed. Inside is a stack of envelopes tied with a piece of twine bleached pale with time.

I sat on the floor and read them all in one night.

They weren't poetic. The handwriting slanted unevenly. They were written in a combination of old-world English and Tagalog.

But they were alive. Each letter was a heartbeat, sentences about train rides and borrowed books, about waiting at stations and promises whispered between duties. About love carried like a lantern through dark years.

They were all addressed to *"My Dearest Eleanor."*

By the time I reached the last one, dated 1951, I felt like I had stolen someone's life.

And I couldn't shake the question.

What happened to them?

It wasn't hard to trace the name.

Eleanor Gatchalian had owned the house once. Records showed she'd passed away five years back, after which her son, who now lived in America, put it up for sale.

The man who wrote the letters, Lemuel Romero, had died even earlier. His return address was a modest two-story in Cainta, which the new owners had converted into a boardinghouse and *sari-sari* store.

But the woman who ran the store gave me the number of Lemuel's grandson. She said he visits once a year at least, mostly during All Souls Day, on his way to the cemetery to pay his respects to Tatay Lemuel.

I hesitate for weeks before reaching out. What do you say to someone about a box of love letters between people who weren't even married to each other?

In the end, I send a message.

Hi. My name is Claire Norieda. I recently bought an old house in Antipolo, and in one of the furniture pieces left behind, I found something I believe belonged to your grandfather, Lemuel. Could we meet?

He replies the next morning. It's a short, direct answer.

Sure. When and where?

We meet at a café in Quezon City, near the university where he teaches.

I expected someone older, maybe more solemn and academic-looking. Instead, Samuel Romero is in his mid-thirties, with a serious face, intense almond-shaped eyes, and dark hair that refuses to stay neat. He looks like he lives half in books, half in constant motion.

"You're Claire Norieda?" he asks as he approaches the table in the quiet corner. I picked it the moment I walked in as not too many people walk past.

"Yes." I get on my feet too quickly, nearly knocking the box of letters over. "You must be Samuel Romero."

He extends a hand. "Sam."

I take it, a little intimidated at his height and the way he's looking at me like I'm a subject he hasn't studied before. His touch is firm and warm as he shakes my hand.

He takes the chair across from mine, the box between us. I lift the lid.

"They're in chronological order," I say. "They're exactly the way I found them in the house at Antipolo."

His hands are careful as he lifts the bundle of envelopes and unties the twine.

"You're from Antipolo, then?" he asks, glancing up from the letters with a curious look.

I shake my head. "Not really, but it's my mother's hometown. She grew up there. When she retired a few years ago, she told me she wanted to live in Antipolo, to be near her sisters. That's how I found Eleanor Gatchalian's house. I guess without my father Metro Manila got a little too much for my mother."

"I'm sorry," he says softly.

"Don't be. My father's gone almost ten years now. He used to work in Ever Gotesco. I grew up in Commonwealth for the most part."

"I'm from Diliman. Second-generation professor, you can say."

"What do you teach?"

"Undergrad History."

I smile, nodding toward the letters in his hands. "These are perfect for you, then. Real pieces of history."

The café noise seems to settle as Sam begins to read. His mouth tightens at some lines, softens at others. When he sets the paper down after nearly an hour, his thumb lingers on the faded ink.

"These were his," he says quietly. "I've only heard about them. I didn't think they'd survived. But I'd know his handwriting anywhere."

"You…knew? About them?"

"Lolo used to tell me stories," he says. "About a beautiful girl whom he loved enough to write every week, even when he had nothing. Even when distance and war kept them apart. That girl was Eleanor."

I swallow hard at the revelation. "Do you know…what happened between them?"

He hesitates before answering. "Eleanor married someone else. Lolo married someone else, too, but it didn't last long. Lola died soon after giving birth to my father. She was a very delicate woman. I have a few pictures of her that I got from Lolo. Eleanor was…someone before. Lolo's first love."

The air changes, heavier with a sadness I didn't expect.

Sam exhales, eyes fixed on the table as he continues. "They loved each other since they were very young. Everyone thought they'd marry. But he was drafted. She waited two years, then her parents arranged a match with another family, wealthier than Lolo's. By the time Lemuel came home, she was already promised. It was too late. Breaking engagements in the old days brought dishonor to the entire family."

My throat tightens. "So they loved each other."

"Yes," he says simply. "But love wasn't enough then."

That should have been the end of it.

But Sam asks if I'd like to help him go through the letters.

"Some of the handwriting's hard to read," he admits. "And I think…their story deserves to be remembered properly. Transcribing the letters electronically would be a good idea. If you've got the time, of course."

We begin meeting every Sunday at the same café.

The first Sunday, I read aloud. Lemuel's words fill the café like echoes from another time.

"My dearest Eleanor, if I could fold the miles between us into this page, I would never let you be lonely again."

I feel heat rise in my chest, though it wasn't me he was writing to.

The second Sunday, we argue.

"Look at this one," Sam says. "He promises her forever, but he had no way to guarantee anything. Isn't that reckless?"

"It's not reckless," I shoot back. "It's brave. Words were all he had."

He laughs at how fierce I sound, then softens. "You'd have believed him, wouldn't you?"

"Yes," I answer haughtily.

"Lolo would have really adored you," he says.

That makes me blush.

The third Sunday, we slip into ease.

Sam volunteers to pick me up from my house in Commonwealth, then rolls into our neighborhood in a silver-black Yamaha.

I don't comment. I only take the helmet he offers me.

At the café, he tells me about his students, who are mostly freshmen and sophomores. I tell him about working for various international schools in the UAE for more than a decade, then coming back home to open my own little preschool and daycare so I could take care of my mother.

Between sips of coffee, we return to the letters.

Another fragment stands out, making us pause.

"Even if the world changes its mind about us, know that I will not change my own. My heart has no other home but you."

My voice falters when I read it. Sam doesn't ask why.

By the fourth Sunday, it's no longer just about Eleanor and Samuel.

"Do you ever think we only find things because we're meant to?" I ask as we pack the letters back into the box.

Sam's hand brushes mine when he hands me the twine.

"Lately," he answers quietly.

When he drops me off at my house, I lean in and kiss his cheek before going inside.

When we reach the final envelope, dated the 14th of February 1951, the café seems hushed, as though it knows.

The handwriting is shaky by then. The letter itself is short.

I hope you are happy, Eleanor.
If he is kind, then I am at peace.
I do not regret loving you. I never will.

I set the page down, my chest aching, my eyes prickling.

"That's it."

Sam nods.

"That's it," he echoes. "A few years later, Lolo met Lola. Then they got married soon after."

"It feels unfair," I whisper.

"Most real stories are," he says. "History is a collection of all that."

I turn to him. "But they loved each other, didn't they? They deserved more."

He's silent for a long time. Then he says, "Maybe their ending isn't ours to fix. But maybe it's a reminder. That sometimes love doesn't survive time. And sometimes…it waits for someone else to carry it forward."

His words hang between us like a fragile bridge.

But when he drops me off, he's the one who kisses me.

A quick peck on the lips.

I don't kiss him back.

That night, I hug the box of letters to my chest and cry myself to sleep.

The next Sunday, Sam comes to my door and rings the bell.

When I open the gate, I see him standing on the pavement in his motorcycle jacket, helmet in one hand, a small maroon envelope in the other.

Without a word, he extends the envelope to me. My name's written on it in bold black marker.

"What's this?" I ask, somewhere between curiosity, surprise, and anxiety.

"Read it," he says. "Please."

I lift the flap and unfold the letter tucked inside. It's handwritten on yellow ruled paper.

My dearest Claire,

I don't know if people still write letters the way Lolo did. Maybe the world moves too fast now. But I've been spending these Sundays with you, and I felt I couldn't let the story of Eleanor and Lemuel go just yet.

Then I realized that it wasn't them I couldn't let go of.

It was you.

So here is my story.

I look forward to Sundays because they mean you. Because visiting the past doesn't feel lonely when you're across the table. Because when I read his words with you, I'm reminded that love isn't only a memory or a part of history.

It's a possibility, here and now.

If Lemuel could write Eleanor every week, then let this be my first letter to you. I hope there will be more.

Yours,

Samuel

My eyes blur before I even reach the end. I lower the page slowly, afraid to breathe too loudly.

He's watching me nervously, vulnerable in a way I hadn't seen before.

"I didn't want Lemuel and Eleanor's story to be the only one that we share," he says softly.

I press my hand over the letter, over my name.

"Thank you," I murmur, reaching out to touch his hand.

He turns his palm so our fingers could tangle.

And when he leans across the space between us, he kisses me.

And I kiss him right back.

It's not rushed. It's not hesitant.

It's just certain.

And it tastes like a beginning, not an ending.

I had the desk moved from Antipolo to the house in Commonwealth.

Now, it rests in a place of honor at the corner of my home office. I always make sure there's a vase of fresh flowers on it, next to a framed photograph of Lemuel taken in the early 1940s. In it, he's dressed in a dark American suit, hair slicked back from his serious face with those familiar intense eyes. He's looking away from the camera, maybe toward his love.

The false drawer is empty now, except for two envelopes. One with Eleanor's name. Lemuel's first letter.

And one with mine. Sam's first letter.

The rest of his Lolo's letters live with Sam now, catalogued and safely kept. Sometimes he shows them to his students, teaching them that history isn't only about wars and treaties, but also about real people.

People who loved, who lost, who left behind paper hearts for strangers to find.

People whose stories never really ended.

Because what I found that night in the desk wasn't the end of Lemuel and Eleanor's love story.

It was the beginning of ours.

CHAPTER 9

A Second-Chance Life

They tell me I should feel grateful.

A second chance. A new life. A heart that beats strong and steady inside my chest when my old one stuttered, failed, and gave up.

Sometimes, gratitude tastes like guilt. Sometimes, I can't sleep without imagining the girl who died so I could live.

I don't know her name. The donor registry doesn't allow that.

But I know I feel her. In the way my breath catches at songs I've never heard before. In the dreams that are not mine. In the strange ache I get when I walk past the pier for the first time after the surgery.

I thought I was going crazy. Until I met him.

⸎

His name is Jay.

He's a barista at this music-themed indie coffee shop I wandered into one afternoon after a panic attack in the hospital parking lot. The kind of place with paintings by local artists on the walls and a small raised platform in the front for open mic nights.

I was hiding in a corner, hands shaking around my cup, when he slid me a small piece of banana bread without a word.

I didn't even look at him until I tasted it.

It was the best banana bread I'd ever had.

And I started crying.

"Hey," he said softly. "It's not that bad."

He had kind eyes. Almost sad.

"I'm sorry," I mumbled, brushing tears off my face. "I just…this tastes like home. And I don't know why. Seriously, though, I've lived in this city my whole life. So…it feels weird."

He didn't laugh. Just tilted his head and said, "Maybe it's reminding you of someone."

And maybe, just maybe, something in me remembered him.

I keep coming back.

Every Tuesday and Thursday, between physical therapy and checkups, I sit in the same corner, drink the same iced coffee, eat the same banana bread he doesn't charge me for.

We start talking.

He's gentle, sometimes funny. He orbits my corner almost protectively, like a bouncer for bad vibes.

He's the kind of boy who never pushes when I'm not ready to talk, but always makes space for whatever I have to share.

I finally tell him I'd had a transplant.

He just nods, like I made perfect sense.

Then one day, he tells me, "My sister loved banana bread. I used to bake it for her every Sunday. I guess the owner here liked it too."

My throat closes.

I don't know why I ask, "What happened to her?"

Because I think…I already know.

He smiles, a small one. His eyes look broken and haunted.

"Car accident," he answers. "Jana signed up to be a donor when she turned eighteen. Said if anything ever happened, she wanted to help someone else live. Lost her last July. I've been on my own since. She kind of raised me."

July.

My hand goes to my chest.

And now, I think he knows too.

"I think I've been looking for you," I say softly.

Jay doesn't cry, but his eyes shimmer in the dim light.

"You feel it too?" he asks. "Sometimes I dream of her. And she's…smiling, but always walking away. I thought I was going crazy. But when I met you, I swear I saw her again."

I nod. "She's still here. Somewhere. And maybe she brought me to you."

He reaches across the table and takes my hand in his. His touch feels warm and soft, like the foam on top of my favorite iced cappuccino.

"I think Jana would be happy," he said. "Knowing her heart found you."

And that's when the weight in my chest lifts.

For the first time since the surgery, I seem to find my heartbeat again.

⁓

We don't fall in love all at once.

It's not cinematic. There are no grand declarations.

Just stolen glances. Just slow, healing conversations.

We share books and music. We take late-night walks at the port, where Jana used to busk during tourist season.

Above all, the simple joy of finding home in someone else's heartbeat.

I tell my doctors I feel stronger. I tell Jay I finally feel real.

I finally feel alive.

Sometimes, he plays his sister's favorite songs on the coffee shop speakers. I dance while helping him mop the floors after closing.

Sometimes, when it's cooler, we sit at the pier and he tells me stories about her.

Sometimes, we don't say anything at all. Just hold each

other, feeling the steady rhythm that once belonged to someone else.

⌀

It's been a year.

I leave the hospital for the last time. No more checkups. No more monitors. Just me, alive and scarred and smiling.

Jay's waiting by the doors with a bouquet of daisies and stargazer lilies in his hand. The same daisies his sister used to draw on his notebooks.

But the lilies…they're all me.

"You ready?" he asks.

I tilt my head, the smile not leaving my face. "For what?"

He grins. "Everything."

I take his hand—and I say the words.

"I love you."

His arms wrap around me, squishing the bouquet a little bit, but I don't mind.

"I love you, too, Cindy."

And my heart—her heart—beats strong.

For the first time, it feels like it's mine.

And I know, wherever she is, she's not gone.

She lives in us.

In our love.

A love we found in banana bread and healing.

A love her heart gave me the chance to find.

And that's the happiest ending I could ever ask for.

CHAPTER 10

The Song to Forever

I REMEMBER EVERYTHING ABOUT HER, EVEN AFTER ALL these years.

She used to sit cross-legged on my floor with her guitar balanced on her thigh, hair falling across her face as she scribbled lyrics into my notebooks.

"Your rhymes suck," Sanya would mutter, chewing on her pen cap.

"And your chords are basic," I'd shoot back, grinning.

But we always finished the song. We always found the hook. We always ended up laughing too hard to care who wrote what.

There was one night when we almost kissed.

Her hand brushed mine on the fretboard, her eyes lingered too long, and the silence between us swelled.

But my phone buzzed, breaking it.

We never talked about it again.

And then…life happened.

College. Gigs in different cities.

Silence.

It's Friday night.

One of the women who work at the radio station with me insists on treating us to a resto-bar in Smallville to celebrate her engagement. The bar she brings us to has a K-pop themed open mic. Neon signs buzz, BTS and Blackpink merch hang around the narrow raised wooden stage like wallpaper, and the smells of fried finger food and light beer linger in the air.

After a quick bite of rice and chicken *inasal,* one of the older technicians says, "Riley, your voice is wasted on news reports. You should sing again."

I laugh him off, but I agree tonight. Half dare, half curiosity. An exception to my usual nights spent alone in the house, strumming chords and humming lyrics no one ever hears.

The host is calling out names when I see her.

Sanya.

Her hair is longer, tied back in a loose ponytail. She's wearing a light blouse, jeans, and that same guitar case slung over her shoulder. She looks a little smaller than I remember, but her eyes are still the same. Expressive, unflinching, full of stories a single pair could ever hold.

She sees me, pausing mid-step toward her table at the corner. "Riley?"

I swallow hard. "Sanya."

She hesitates for a moment, just holding my gaze with

hers. When she finally opens her mouth, she says, "How…how are you?"

"I'm fine," I manage to force out. "You?"

Up close, she looks tired. "Fine. You still work for the radio station?"

I nod. "Yeah. Still at the call center?"

She nods, then after a beat of silence, "It was nice seeing you here."

"Same," I say quickly.

She retreats to her table without another word.

⌒

Deeper into the night, the host asks for volunteers to sing the latest hits from *K-pop Demon Hunters.*

A group of college girls sitting next to our table nudge each other, whispering and pointing at me. One even waves.

"Manong Riley! You should sing! I heard you sing once at the Miss Dinagyang pre-pageant!"

I force a smile, but shake my head. I would burn in hell before they can make me sing 'Soda Pop' in public.

Sanya appears at my shoulder, eyebrow raised.

"Fan club?" she teases.

"Listeners," I mutter. "Occupational hazard."

She chuckles. It hits me how much I missed that sound.

"One more song?" she asks so softly I almost miss it.

I stare at her in surprise. "What do you have in mind? I don't exactly have the vocal range for 'Golden.'"

She smirks. "No. 'Free.'"

I hesitate. I've played it more than a few times on air… but to actually sing it?

"C'mon, Riley," says Sanya. "I'm sure you've got one more song in you."

And just like always, I can't say no.

❧

The first strum of her guitar makes my chest ache.

When she starts singing, the resto-bar falls quiet. Her voice is richer now, deeper from the years she has lived, but it still twines around mine like it was made to.

The crowd perks up instantly. Some squeal, others sway. The college girls bounce up and down their seats as they take videos with their phones.

Halfway through, I look at Sanya, and she's already looking at me.

Her lips curve mid-lyric—and I feel it again, after so many years of silence.

When she sings *"I just wanna be free,"* it doesn't feel like any old verse. It feels like a confession.

A secret no one else knows.

By the final chorus, people are waving their cellphones in the air as if in an actual concert. But all I feel is Sanya's voice pressed against mine, the old fire rekindled in the neon lights of a narrow wooden stage.

It feels as if no years have passed at all. Her harmonies wrap around my melody. My verses answer her lines.

And when our eyes meet, it's electric.

Half nostalgia, half something new.

❧

We win the loudest applause of the night.

Sanya rolls her eyes, but I see the flush in her cheeks.

"That was…" I start.

"Embarrassing?" she finishes. "Corny?"

"Perfect," I say, shaking my head.

"We wish," she intones.

We laugh awkwardly, and it's like the years collapse.

We step off the stage to cheers. Two of the college girls rush over.

"Manong Riley, you're so good!" one gushes. "You should post reels of yourself singing. You'll go viral in no time!"

"Is she your girlfriend?" the other teases, giggling, nudging her friend as they both eye Sanya.

I chuckle as I back away. "Uh…thanks for listening. Tag me in your videos, okay?"

Sanya snorts, pulling me aside. "Wow. Still the heartthrob."

"You jealous?" I ask, grinning.

She scoffs. "Of course not."

But the faint color on her face and neck says otherwise.

"Can I drop you home?" I offer, before I can stop myself.

After a pause, she nods.

❧

I say goodnight to my colleagues, then lead Sanya to my car parked down the curb. It's a modest white sedan, a little old but kept impeccably clean.

She places her guitar case on the backseat without a word.

When we drive out of the resto-bar's parking lot, the city is still alive with taxis, night shift workers, and vendors selling fishball and *balut*.

"So," I say, "how's call center life?"

She shrugs. "Pays the bills. Keeps my dad's meds covered for the most part. Music's…still here, though. Gigs here and there, on my nights off. The bar's been nice to me for years now. I was their first acoustic night after the pandemic."

I smile at her as we pause at a red light. "You never stopped. That's nice to hear."

"Did you?"

"I traded late-night jams for graveyard shifts at the station."

She tilts her head at me. "You were always very good, you know. You could have been the next Rico Blanco."

"You were better," I counter. "The next Juris, perhaps."

She laughs, shaking her head. "You always said that."

We fall into silence. The kind that stretches but doesn't break.

Finally, as we drive down the highway toward her house in Pavia, I say it.

"I thought of you a lot over the years. More than I should have."

She sighs. "Come on, Riley. We outgrew all of that."

"No, listen. I don't care how many years passed. I never forgot you. I never forgot us."

"Riley, don't. Just don't."

"Why not?" I shoot back, gripping the wheel a little too tightly.

When she doesn't answer, I pull over to the shoulder and switch on the hazard lights.

We sit in the dark, heavy silence.

"Why not, Sanya?" I ask again. "Just let me know. I won't bother you again. I'll take you home and you won't ever see me after this."

A sob escapes her.

The sound makes my entire body clench.

"Because I thought of you, too, you idiot," she chokes out brokenly.

"Sanya, I—"

"Oh, shut up, you don't know anything!" she exclaims. "I thought you forgot about me."

Then she hurls herself into my arms.

Cᴏ

We end up at my place.

I drive to Alta Tierra, to the old bungalow I inherited from my parents. I don't let go of her hand through the entire journey.

As soon as we're through the door, she kicks off her shoes and settles on the same old carpet in the living room, guitar in hand. I remember how my mother would always keep it spotless for Sanya.

With barely any effort, she starts strumming, humming along to a new, gentle, but melancholic sound.

"You kept writing," I say. "This sounds like something you would come up with."

"You didn't," she accuses.

I smile crookedly. "I lost the words when you left."

Her strumming stops. Our eyes lock. The silence that settles between us is not hollow, but charged and dangerous.

And then I move.

I cross the room in a few strides. I take the guitar from her lap, then set it gently aside. She doesn't stop me. Her breath catches when I sit beside her, close enough to feel her warmth.

"Riley—" she starts.

But I kiss her.

It's not careful. It's not polite. It's the kiss we should have had years ago, pulled taut and raw by time.

Her lips part against mine. My hands cup her jaw, sliding into her hair, pulling her closer. She sighs softly, as if in surrender, and it sets me on fire.

Her mouth tastes like honey and daring. Mine must taste like hunger, because she gasps, bites my lip, then kisses me harder.

She climbs onto my lap, straddling me, her hands fumbling with my shirt. My body reacts instantly, heat flooding, until I'm drowning in the music that is her.

We break only to breathe, lips still brushing.

"Sing with me again, Sanya," I murmur. "Please."

"Then stay with me," she answers breathlessly.

And the night stretches, our duet turning into something without words, something we both swore we'd buried but never stopped needing.

When dawn creeps in, she's asleep against my chest, covered in my thin blue blanket.

I trace her hairline gently, whispering against her cheek the words I never got to say all those years ago.

"One more song, Sanya. Always one more."

But this time, I know we'll sing it together.

Forever.

CHAPTER 11

Days of Flowers

THE COLLEGE DISTRICT IS LOUD EVEN IN THE mornings.

Jeepneys honk, students spill onto sidewalks with earbuds in, tricycle and pedicab drivers yell routes. The world around me doesn't seem to stop moving.

But at *Kapehan sa Kilid*, at my corner table by the glass, it's quiet. My ritual is a cup of fresh *barako*, behind the day's newspaper I don't always read.

And the view from the window.

Always the window.

It started as habit after retirement. The doctors said to keep a routine, or I'd lose myself in the empty silence of the house. The *kapehan* became my watchpost.

Every morning, I walk from my bungalow with its garden full of aloe vera pots and *santan* beds, then I take my usual seat.

I sip the coffee they serve me without asking what I want anymore.

I breathe.

And then, one May morning, I see her.

A new flower shop, just across the street. Buckets of roses, bundles of daisies and baby's breath, white *sampaguita* glowing like pearls in the sun.

And her, tying colorful paper around stems with ribbons, brushing long black hair from her forehead with the back of her wrist.

She looks younger than me by maybe ten to fifteen years. Early forties, if I try to guess. Not married. There's no ring on her finger, as far as I can see.

She smiles at customers in a way that doesn't look forced. The students and the young professionals all love her.

I don't mean to watch. But after years of watching only shadows and exits, I find myself watching her instead.

Lila.

That's what the *kapehan*'s owner called her once, when she sent across a small bouquet of pink roses for the counter as her way of greeting her new neighbors.

The name fit perfectly.

The first time she reaches out, it startles me.

It's a white daisy, tucked into my newspaper by Roque, the young man who always brings my coffee and newspaper.

"What's this?" I ask.

He grins. "From Miss Lila, boss."

Once Roque makes his way back to the counter, I lift the flower, breathing in the softness.

When I look up, I find her already waiting, half-hidden behind a bucket of red roses.

I should look away.

Instead, I nod, pressing the daisy to my chest.

Her smile lights something in me I thought had burned out years ago.

* * *

It becomes our kind of language.

She sends *gumamela, sampaguita,* and roses. Roque winks at me as though he's the brains behind this entire operation.

On the fifth day, I cross the street.

"Miss Lila," I say. My voice comes out rougher than I remember. "You giving flowers to every man in the *kapehan?*"

She looks up at me, eyes amused yet assessing. She radiates an affable yet dangerously sharp air that befits a Secretary of Defense.

"Only the ones who look like they'd know how to keep them alive," she answers without hesitation.

I actually laugh. For the first time in years, it doesn't sound strange in my own throat.

"Alfred Rivero," I tell her, lowering my head slightly as I extend a hand. "Retired Army Major. At your service."

"Lila Dos Santos," she said. "Former events coordinator. HoneyBee Blossoms."

Her hand is small, but her grip is firm as she shakes mine.

I don't want to let go.

☙

I make a habit of waiting for her in the evenings, watching as she closes up.

She sweeps petals into her dustpan, then rearranges buckets so they wouldn't topple overnight. I take her bags and walk her to her house at the end of the street. We don't even touch, but she always waves me off, watching from behind her gate as I make my way back down the narrow road.

A month later, I start waiting for her in the mornings too. I take her bags and quietly keep pace with her as she walks. I help her open the doors to her shop. I bring her coffee from across the street.

One night, she tells me that she left Manila because the cutthroat attitude of the corporate world was not for her anymore. She felt too old, too worn out.

She wanted something slower, something more real. A fresh, gentler start, just like the flowers she'd always loved.

Students and regulars whisper that the old soldier at the *kapehan* was in love with the flower lady.

Maybe they are right.

One evening, I carry something new with me.

Not a weapon, not a file, not a report. Not the only things I know how to carry.

For the first time, I carry a bouquet.

Rare blooms I asked a contact from Davao to send up: jade vine, fiery red anthurium, orchids pale as moonlight. Strange and beautiful together, tied with purple ribbons that feel like velvet to the touch.

When she finally locks up her shop and turns, I'm there.

She stares at the bouquet in surprise.

"For me?" she asks.

"For you," I answer. My voice almost fails me, but I push through. "A gift."

She touches an anthurium, almost reverently. "What are they for?"

I clear my throat. "I wanted to give you something real. Something strong. Something that endures."

I see it then. The barest hint of a smile on her lips. "And?"

I swallow the lump in my throat. I clench my stomach muscles as if anticipating a blow.

"Something that survives," I continue, "and blooms even more beautifully."

Her hand lingers on the bouquet. Her other hand slips into mine.

"Then I'll take them," she says softly. "And I'll take you."

I lean down and, at long last, kiss her.

I kiss her gently, but with certainty.

I kiss her slowly, because I had waited long enough to be sure this love can really grow.

The tricycles and pedicabs rattle by. Students spill out of stores and eateries and internet shops, laughing. The world keeps moving around us.

But for the first time in years, I feel still. Rooted.

Maybe my routine has finally found its meaning—across the street, in her arms, in this kiss that means something new is blooming.

The years blur after that, in the way only the best years do.

Every morning, I still sit by the *kapehan* window with my *barako* and newspaper.

But now there's a vase on every table too. Vases that never run empty, always filled with wild sprays of *gumamela*, white and bright daisies, or a colorful riot of roses.

And when I look up from the print, she's there.

My Lila.

Pouring sugar into her own cup, humming under her breath, her hair loose around her face, the strands now threaded through with hints of silver.

My beautiful flower lady.

My wife.

My smile and laughter after the long, hollow years of silence.

It was only during our wedding night when I found out why she sent me all those flowers in the first place.

They meant it was never too late for our kind of love to bloom.

ABOUT THE AUTHOR

Shirley Siaton writes edgy and evocative novels and poems. Her worlds are in a deliciously dark cross-section of the romance, neo-noir, action, contemporary, and fantasy genres. Her background in various Asian martial arts inspires a lot of her work.

She has several books of fiction and poetry released since February 2023. Her first book is the free verse collection *Black Cat and other poems. Befallen* (March 2025) is her first full-length novel. She also pens juvenile literature as Shirley Parabia.

She is an award-winning writer, poet, and journalist in English, Filipino, and Hiligaynon. Her essays, short stories, and poems have been published internationally in print and digital media. Her multi-lingual plays have been staged in the Philippines.

Shirley is a black belt in Shotokan Karate and an international certified fitness coach. She has a Master's degree in Public Administration and works in education, wellness, and publishing. Originally from Iloilo City, she lives in the Middle East with her husband and two daughters.

ON THE WEB

Shirley's official website:
shirleysiaton.com

Complete reading guide:
shirley.pub

Subscribe to Shirley's VIP list for free exclusive updates:
newsletter.shirleysiaton.com